THE GAMBLER'S DAUGHTER

THE GAMBLER'S DAUGHTER

BY SHIRLEE SMITH MATHESON

DUNDURN PRESS
TORONTO

Editor: Joy Gugeler
Cover and interior design and production: Teresa Bubela, Joy Gugeler
Cover illustration by Barbara Munzar

Library and Archives Canada Cataloguing in Publication

Matheson, Shirlee Smith
    The gambler's daughter / by Shirlee Smith Matheson.

ISBN 978-1-55002-718-1

    I. Title.

PS8576.A823G35 2009   jC813'.54   C2009-900819-X

Canadä

We acknowledge the support of the **Canada Council for the Arts** and the **Ontario Arts Council** for our publishing program. We also acknowledge the financial support of the **Government of Canada** through the **Book Publishing Industry Development Program** and **The Association for the Export of Canadian Books**, and the **Government of Ontario** through the **Ontario Book Publishers Tax Credit program**, and the **Ontario Media Development Corporation**.

Care has been taken to trace the ownership of copyright material used in this book. The author and the publisher welcome any information enabling them to rectify any references or credits in subsequent editions.

J. Kirk Howard, President

Printed and bound in Canada.
www.dundurn.com

Dundurn Press
3 Church Street, Suite 500
Toronto, Ontario, Canada
M5E 1M2

Gazelle Book Services Limited
White Cross Mills
High Town, Lancaster, England
LA1 4XS

Dundurn Press
2250 Military Road
Tonawanda, NY
U.S.A. 14150

My heart is pounding so loudly I don't hear the lock rattle, or see the door bulge under the weight of outside pressure. Suddenly the latch gives and the door is flung wide open. The wind from outside fans the flame in the lamp, and it sputters and dies. Moonlight casts a shadow and silhouettes the broad shoulders of a man standing in the door frame.

"Teddy!" I half yell in warning.

"Shush! Do you want to wake the whole neighbourhood?" a familiar voice growls.

The door slams and we pause for a moment, each breathless.

'Bean-Trap' Braden, my stepfather, leans panting against the door. I wait, my pounding heart and his heavy breathing pulsing in the darkness.

"What's wrong?" I whisper, reaching across in the dark for Teddy's hand.

He flares a match as he comes over to our beds. I can see, by the dim light, that his hair is mussed, sticking up like porcupine quills. He pushes it back from his face with shaking hands.

"It's okay, Loretta," he says. "I've had a bit of trouble. Nothing to worry about. They've got to know that Bean-Trap Braden is a man to be reckoned with." He manages a bit of a smile as he looks down at me, then over at my brother, Teddy, asleep in the cot next to mine.

"Earlier tonight I heard a gunshot. I think someone was aiming at the cabin!" I whisper accusingly.

"What! I didn't hear...."

"Just before you came. A shot...on the wall outside."

He strides to the door and opens it a crack, his revolver cocked as he peers into the darkness. No sound, except for an owl and the alert bark of a dog.

He closes the door again, and shoves a knife in the frame to keep it barred. "We'll check it out in the morning. Now get some sleep. I'm going to stay up for a while. I'll keep the lamp low."

Bean-Trap Braden is a big man, tall as a grizzly bear, with wide shoulders and strong arms and hands. As he sits in the dark I think of him each morning when he combs his hair straight back, long, thick and wavy, trims and waxes his curled mustache, and examines his big teeth, rimmed and backed with gold. I feel safe, somehow, to have such a formidable guard defending us.

I hear him mutter a sequence of numbers as

he counts the money from the moose hide bag he's dumped onto the table.

"Will we have to move again?" I ask from my bed in the dark corner.

"No, honey, not for a while. But when we do, we'll be together. I won't leave you and Teddy alone again." His chair scrapes back. He walks over to the stove, lifts the lid and pokes at the embers. "Maybe I should ask one of Pete and Millie's kids to stay with you at night. They have a couple of boys who could keep an eye on the place."

"Maybe they can lend us one of their dogs...."

"Good idea!" he said, inspired again. "I'll talk to Pete tomorrow. He's got a nice big Husky that's good with kids. She'll protect you like you're her own pups. No one would try to cross *her*."

Millie and Pete LaFont are a Sikanni Indian family–the only neighbours we've met here. Millie was kind to me when we first arrived. She helped me clean the shack and taught me how to use the old wood stove.

I fall asleep, confident that Bean-Trap, and Pete's and Millie's Husky dog, will keep us safe. Being babysat by a dog–Teddy will love that. Maybe I can use it for a story tomorrow, when we do our lessons.

♦ ♦ ♦

The next morning, we all go outside to check

the cabin walls for gunshot holes. Teddy likes playing detective too, even if he doesn't know what we're looking for.

"If it was a .22, the bullets would be small and the wood would close up around them," Bean-Trap explains. Noticing Teddy's frightened look, he quickly adds, "But I *know* it wasn't a bullet. Likely a bird hit the wall, or a pine cone dropped off that big tree." He sounds convinced but I'm not so sure.

Bean-Trap walks across to Pete's cabin, and the two men return a few minutes later with a beautiful white Husky.

"Her name is *Mika we*" Pete says. "It means 'the mother' in Cree."

"Miki!" Teddy says, and squats to pet her. She licks his hand, and I hold out mine so she can nuzzle it. Miki is only my second friend in Weasel City. Suddenly I realize how lonely I've been and feel grateful for the company, animal or not.

When Bean-Trap goes to work, we lead Miki on a rope and walk down to the river for our lesson. She lays on the bank, happy to sit in on our class. I get Teddy started doing penmanship exercises, rows of circles and jagged lines, in preparation for copying out the alphabet. Next he sounds out all the letters, and practices three-letter words like "cat" and "dog."

By mid-afternoon, I begin to feel kind of dizzy, and wonder if the late autumn sun is hotter than it seems. A film of sweat has formed on my upper lip and along my hairline. My stomach feels queasy and I think I might be sick.

"Let's go back to the house Teddy," I say putting my papers back into my satchel and clambering up the river bank.

"Aw, do we have to?" Teddy reluctantly picks up his papers and pencils, and we lead Miki back along the trail.

The afternoon passes slowly. Teddy works on a printing lesson, and some arithmetic. He's amazing with numbers.

By suppertime I'm feeling faint and have to lie down. "Teddy, check the bread in the oven for me if I fall asleep. I put it in half an hour ago."

"Okay," he says, absorbed in his exercises.

I doze off for an hour and when I wake up Millie is there, heating the kettle on the stove for a pot of tea. She checks the oven. My bread is ready and perfect. When the three loaves cool a bit she cuts some end-slices, lathers them with butter and honey, and takes them on a plate to Teddy and the kids who are playing outside with a ball, and a bat that Pete has carved from a tree branch.

When she comes back in she looks at me with concern, her head cocked to one side like Miki's. She comes over to the bed and takes my hair in her hands, starting to brush it. For some reason, tears well up in my eyes. No one has brushed my hair since my mother died.

Millie talks softly to me in her native language,

Sikanni, and I explain why I'm crying, in English. Even though we don't speak the same language, and it sounds like we're just babbling, we understand each other and laugh at our exaggerated body language. I use my hands as much as my tongue to describe things, and she stops brushing my hair to "demonstrate" her conversation.

She indicates a circle, big, round, like a cycle, and then cups her hands like a sun or moon, points to herself, then to me. Oh, words! If only I knew what she was saying.

"Every moon, we dance," she says, smiling.

I'm not sure what she means by this, but I am determined to keep our conversation going. I'm feeling better now that I've eaten, so I continue, slowly unwinding the story of our arrival in Weasel City. Millie listens, stroking and brushing my hair.

"I was born in Portland, Oregon. My name wasn't Loretta Braden then, it was Benedictson. I lived there with my mother and grandmother. When I got old enough, Grandma Benedictson took me for walks in the park and told me stories about my father who built big ships in the dockyards there. He was killed in an accident when I was five. A crane broke on the work site and crushed him under the hull of a ship."

I barely remember him, but the stories Grandma and Mom told helped me feel better, just as telling mine to Millie, now, helps. I plunge on, hoping she understands more than a few words.

"Mom tried to get work in Oregon as a school teacher, but the only job she was offered was in Fairbanks, Alaska, so we had to move.

"We arrived in Fairbanks just before Christmas and tried to settle in. One afternoon when Mom and I were on our way home, struggling with arms full of groceries, Mom fell on the ice. A man came running to our rescue, picked up the fallen groceries, and brought us home. That's how we met William J. Braden, otherwise known as 'Bean-Trap.'

"That Christmas Bean-Trap came to the door dragging an enormous tree which barely fit in the house. He lifted me up to put the star on the top branch and gave me whisker-rubs that made me laugh when his chin brushed against my cheek. He told funny stories about prospectors and pilots, trappers and fur traders, men he knew from all over the North. He gave Mom and me a beautiful coat, made by the wives of some of the trappers he knew.

"That summer, he paid for us to take a boat trip back to Portland to visit my Grandmother. She was very ill, and we knew this might be our last visit. She died a few months later.

"When Mom and Bean-Trap married six months after that, we moved to Eagle in north-eastern Alaska, where Bean-Trap had some gold claims. In winter, Eagle looks just like a Christmas card village. The mountains, trees, frozen lakes and rivers, are all white and shine like diamonds.

"Our house was a skid-shack, a little two-room place that rested on logs so it could be moved to new claims. While we were in Eagle, Teddy was born. Suddenly I had a baby brother!

"One night when Mom and I were sitting up and Teddy was asleep in his crib, she asked if I could ever call Bean-Trap 'Dad'.

"I said 'But my own dad...I can't forget *him!*'"

"She said she didn't want me to do that, but he was gone and Bean-Trap was like a new dad in his place. She said he loved me like his own child. I said I'd think about it and she never asked me about it again."

My expression changes and Millie expects something in the story is about to go wrong. She looks at me quizzically.

"One night, as we all lay asleep, we heard three gun-shots–a trouble warning! We flung open the door to see the sky bursting into red flames and people running from their cabins, grabbing dishpans and buckets. Everyone began scooping up snow to throw onto the flames, but it was no use."

I remember the scene so vividly: before anyone could get near it, the gambling house exploded like a firecracker, shooting thousands of red stars into the night sky. Hours later, the embers still glowed and the walls smouldered, charred wood hissing into the frozen ground.

Then the crowd began to talk about Bean-

Trap and his 'real' business, the one that brought him a lot more money than his gold claims. One man threw down his bucket and lumbered back to his cabin mumbling that it was too bad Bean-Trap hadn't been inside.

I started to cry, but Mom consoled me, saying they didn't really mean it, that it wasn't him they hated–just what he did for a living. They hated to be tempted. They hated to lose.

At the time I thought it was their own fault; after all, Bean-Trap didn't drag them in to play cards. They had *wanted* to be there.

Now, I realize that the gambling house Bean-Trap ran took gold and wages away from the miners and fur money from the trappers, leaving their families with no food for the winter. When men give in to temptation, their wives and children suffer too. They put their cabins up for bets, their mineral claims, even the clothes on their backs. Bean-Trap had a huge collection of guns, boots, and coats because they gave up anything they had to keep gambling.

They were mean and angry that night, but their anger was really only another kind of fire, but just as dangerous.

"The fire changed everything," I say to Millie after a long silence. "When the gambling house burned down we had to leave Eagle. Bean-Trap lost money and Mom lost her teaching job. Parents wouldn't send their kids to her classes because of her connection to Bean-Trap. Kids pushed me around on my way to and from school, and wouldn't play with me at recess.

"My friend, Jana, even passed me a note in class that said, 'We can't be frends any more. Sory.' I wrote back, asking why, but she just replied, 'Becuz you are the gamblers dotter.' I ripped her note into tiny pieces, but I can still see it, spelling mistakes and all.

"We moved back to Fairbanks. Bean-Trap said he had to plan his next business venture. He was restless. We were running out of money. Mom got an anxious look on her face every time she went to the bank or the grocery store. Bean-Trap wanted to stake more claims, but he wasn't a prospector. We knew he'd go somewhere to open up a new gambling house, and that we might not see him for months.

"During those cold winter nights, Mom grew very sick. I was scared; we had no money for a doctor and we didn't know anybody who could help us for free. Bean-Trap didn't want people to get to know us in case they got suspicious. So, I nursed Mom as well as I could and bought some food with the money that Bean-Trap sent to us every so often from wherever his 'claims' were, but I knew I had to do something before Mom's condition got worse. Her coughing sometimes went on all night, and she soon grew too weak to even get out of bed.

"One night, when it was forty-six degrees below zero, I put on my coat and boots, told

Teddy to look after Mom, and walked a mile to
the hospital. I was nearly frozen when I arrived,
but I managed to tell them about Mom. The doctor,
nurse and I drove back to our house in their car.
"Mom was taken to the hospital by ambulance
that night, Good Friday. She died Easter Sunday,
of pneumonia." I start to cry again, sobbing into
Millie's shoulder as I remember how horrible I felt
when I realized Teddy and I were alone.

"We had no idea where Bean-Trap had gone.
The welfare people came in and moved us to a
foster home until they finally managed to contact
him. He arranged for us to travel by river and
pack trail across part of Alaska, and the Yukon,
to join him here in British Columbia!

"We arrived in Fort Nelson in June. Bean-Trap
was delayed on business out of town, so we waited
for him in the town's only hotel. While we were
there, Teddy and I met a boy my age named Jay
Smith and his friend, Bugs, as well as Jay's
famous pilot uncle, "Midnight" Smith, and
Midnight's pilots Cannonball and Bud."

My voice gets stern when I remember Bean-
Trap marching into the hotel room, scooping us
up, full of wild news and big plans.

"When Bean-Trap met Jay Smith, he had a
violent reaction. 'You kin to Jed Smith?' he said,
shoving his unshaven face into Jay's. That's when
we discovered that Jay's father, Jed Smith, was
the man who'd set fire to Bean-Trap's gambling
place in Eagle!

"Without even saying thank-you to Jay for his kindness to us in Fort Nelson, he grabbed Teddy and threw him over his shoulder and ordered me to follow. I was so embarrassed! 'Don't you ever have anything to do with that kid again, you hear? The Smiths, all their kin–even that famous bush pilot brother–they're all our sworn enemies! And don't ever forget it!'

"Bean-Trap doesn't know it, but I have written to Jay since coming to live in this log cabin in Weasel City. I described it to him as 'the loneliest settlement in the world'. Once I started, I just had to tell him everything. Well, almost.

"But that's another story," I say to Millie. She smiles, knowing I will tell her the rest later. She has brushed my hair to a blond sheen and braided it while I was talking. She doesn't say much in response, but I know she understands. Perhaps it won't be so lonely here after all.

Millie winds the two braids around my head, securing them with pins taken from her own hair. I go to look in a mirror. I hardly recognize myself! I look so much older!

◆   ◆   ◆

Bean-Trap comes in, late. He's whistling under his breath so I know the evening must have gone well. I hear a thunk as he tosses the money bag onto the table. I know where he keeps his money hidden, at least I know a few of the spots.

He wanders over to my bed to check on me.

"Oh, Loretta! You're still awake? It's almost two in the morning."

"I know. I was asleep but I heard you come in."

He comes over to the bed. "Are you okay? You look pale. Did someone come here, hassle you?"

"No, I just felt a bit sick this afternoon and Millie came over to make me tea and talk. I think it'll be all right here," I say with a weak smile, "as long as the shooting stops."

"It will," Bean-Trap says. "Well, goodnight."

He goes over to his bed on the far side of the room. In a few minutes *he's* snoring, but *I'm* wide awake.

"What's for lunch, Loretta? I'm starving."

I'd made bread yesterday, and we had some cold meat and hard cheddar cheese. I open a can of peaches and set out some raisin cookies I'd baked. As Teddy, Bean-Trap and I gather around the table, it seems hard to believe the summer's almost over. We've been in Weasel City for three months already; we moved from Fort Nelson in June, 1942.

We'd journeyed forty miles up the Muskwa River to Weasel City, a real joke considering it's anything but a city! A few trappers' cabins are scattered along Kledo Creek where it flows into the Muskwa River, and we have a small a fur-trading post, but that's it.

Now that I'm fourteen, I'm responsible for doing the cooking, the laundry, and trying to keep our old one-room log cabin clean. Bean-Trap told me that this cabin was once the home of two trappers, Henry Courvosier and Bert

Sheffield, who staged the Great Fort Nelson Fur Robbery on July 12, 1936. They tied up the traders and stole twenty-nine bales of fur valued at thirty-two thousand dollars! I suppose we should feel privileged to live in such a historic house!

Besides doing all the housework, I'm teaching Teddy, who's almost six now, how to read and write.

"Loretta's showing me how to count," Teddy volunteers, between mouthfuls of bread.

Bean-Trap lifts one eyebrow. "You know how to count, boy! I taught you how, a long time ago." He picks up a worn deck of cards and starts shuffling it at the table, then flips the cards so fast they become a blur.

"Six of hearts! Seven of diamonds! Ace of spades!" Teddy sings out in time to his lightning-fast hand.

"Gimme a straight flush, boy!"

"Five cards, same suit! Five, six, seven, eight, nine!" Teddy chimes.

"Full House!"

"Three of a kind, one pair."

"Gimme one!"

"King, king, king, eight, eight!"

My head spins.

He throws down an eight of hearts and a two of spades, and booms, "Two from eight!"

"Six!"

"Eight plus two!"

"Ten!"

Bean-Trap rocks back triumphantly on the two hind legs of his chair. "See, he's a smart little fella, Loretta," he says proudly. "He can run numbers backwards and forwards. So, what were you trying to teach him?"

I smile weakly. "One plus one...."

"Oh, he's way past that. Tell you what, though. I think he's ready to learn multiplying. Teach him that. And his goes-in-to's."

"Dividing?" I ask.

"Yeah, dividing. He's gonna be my banker some day, and you can be my manager. I'm going to need people I can trust with my money. Now, how about reading? He knows numbers when he sees them, but he don't know his letters. Gotta learn letters. We have any books around here?" He twists around on his chair and pulls out some magazines from the orange-crate. "Oops, guess these are too old for him."

"What?" Teddy leans forward, as curious as ever. Bean-Trap whisks the magazines from his sight, but not before I see a picture of a woman in a bathing suit.

Bean-Trap laughs. "Old Henry must have left these here. See what else you can find."

"There's a Bible," I say hesitantly.

"A Bible? Good! Should be lots of words in there he can learn. Start him off with something interesting, like the whale story. He'll like that!"

"The whale?" Teddy asks, eyes wide.

"Yeah, you see, there's this old guy named Jonah. God asks Jonah to go to the city and tell everyone who lives there to shape up because they're a bad bunch. Jonah, he don't see why it's his job to be God's messenger, so he runs off to sea instead."

Teddy's eyes are fixed on Bean-Trap, who gets up and paces the cabin floor to continue the tale, using wild expressions and hand signals.

"Then this fierce storm comes up, like an Alaskan coast williwaw. The wind's blowing and the sea's crashing, waves high as houses, fistfuls of rain's tossing down, and that boat's bouncing around like a flea on a dog's back." Bean-Trap's arms are waving frantically as he imitates sailors stumbling about on the ship's rolling deck. I laugh as Teddy joins in, another wobbly sailor.

"Finally, the sailors figure there must be a reason for this; maybe God's mad at someone on board. The captain makes everyone on the ship 'fess up. Jonah admits he's on the lam, running from God because he's disobeyed orders. When the sailors hear this, they throw him overboard to protect themselves.

"Quick as a snap, he's gobbled up by a big whale swimming behind the ship, waiting for some tasty morsel to drop off the deck."

"He fell off the deck and got ate by a whale?"

"Yesiree-bob! And you know what happened then?"

"No, what?" Teddy asks eagerly.

Bean-Trap comes back to the table and squats down next to Teddy. "You'll hafta learn to read to find out! Loretta, where's that old Bible? Find the Book of Jonah. I think you've got yourself an A-1 student."

Bean-Trap stands looking very satisfied with himself, stomach thrust out, picking his teeth with an ivory toothpick that suddenly resembles a sliver of whale's tooth.

"Come on, Teddy. Help me with the dishes, then we'll start our reading lesson," I say.

Teddy jumps up excitedly to gather the plates and cups. Bean-Trap winks at me and I smile back. Maybe he's turning over a new leaf.

"Gotta go to work," Bean-Trap says.

I almost laugh. 'Work,' that's a good one. His nickname is "Bean-Trap" because he traps other men's "beans," which is what they call money around here. We found out the hard way that his 'work' can get us all into a lot of trouble. We're in Weasel City right now is because he is "fading from the scene" for a while.

After Bean-Trap leaves I sit down with Teddy at our oilcloth-covered board table. I lay out two pieces of blank paper, and the dusty mouse-chewed Bible left behind by Henry or Bert. When I open the Bible, a smell like old socks wafts out. "Whew! Henry must have kept this stuck in an old boot!" I laugh. Teddy laughs too, and we settle in to our studies.

"Okay, this is the alphabet." I have written the

twenty-six symbols, in capitals and small letters, across the top of a page. "And here's how they sound...."

An hour later, Teddy can write JONAH and WHALE, and recognize these words in the Bible. I am amazed we're making such fast progress!

About supper time, a knock sounds at the door. I stiffen, uncertain as to who it might be. Maybe it's someone angry with Bean-Trap, someone who's lost his summer's gold and is coming to raid the house! I warn Teddy to stay back. With a pounding heart, I walk to the door and peep through a crack between the door and the frame. It's Millie!

I open the door and beckon her inside. She enters, smiling shyly, accompanied by her youngest son, Harold, who clings onto her skirt and hides behind her legs. She holds out a cloth-covered tray. I lift back the cloth and there are a dozen cinnamon buns, their raisin, walnut and brown sugar centres oozing sweetness and a heavenly smell.

I flash her a broad, thankful smile, and offer her a chair. Harold is eyeing a leftover dish of peaches. "You can have them," I say, and give him a spoon.

Millie notices the letters that Teddy has printed in squiggly lines on his paper. She points at them and looks questioningly at me. I nod. She points to the letters and then to herself. She wants me to teach her too! But how can I teach her to read when she speaks only a few words of English and I can't speak Sikanni? Then I get an idea: the trading post manager, Mr. Benton, can speak both languages. I'll ask him to write out a dozen words in each language, and we can start from there.

"I'm going to be a real teacher, Teddy!" I say, nodding at Millie, "and you won't be the only kid in school anymore!"

Millie and Pete have six kids, ranging in age from one to sixteen. None has learned to read or write, although Pete and the older boys can speak some English. Their two girls are one and three; this little guy is two.

The older boys are always working with their Dad out on the trapline, or chopping wood, or hunting. Teddy sometimes plays with Ernie and Pat, the eight- and ten-year-old boys, but Bean-Trap has instructed us to never stray far from the cabin, so Teddy can't go hunting or fishing with them. He doesn't want us to become too friendly with the neighbours, but because Pete doesn't gamble, we can at least associate with his family safely.

Bean-Trap's customers aren't usually Native people; not only because they don't have as much money as the others, but because the police, the priest, the Indian Agent, and the traders would all raise the roof if they thought Bean-Trap was encouraging them to become customers. No one seems to care what other miners or trappers do–they can drink moonshine, gamble, or shoot each other for all anyone cares. And sometimes they do.

After Millie leaves, I decide to prepare the next lessons for my two new students. An hour later, a sharp crack resounds against the cabin wall. I jump from my chair, and Teddy and I hide in a shadowed corner. We wait and wait, but the sound doesn't repeat itself, not that I could hear it above my thundering heartbeat.

"Do you think someone's after us, Loretta?" Teddy asks. His voice quavers and his eyes open wide in fright.

"I don't think so. It was likely a stray pellet–kids out shooting at squirrels or birds."

"It's nearly dark!" Teddy whispers, fear mounting in his voice.

"We'll check it out in the morning when the sun's up, when Bean-Trap is home," I say, trying to reassure him. "We'll look for marks on the log wall. If we find something, we'll tell him. He'll make sure it won't happen again."

"I'm scared, Loretta. What if people start to hate us here, like in Eagle when they set fire...."

"Sshhh. Come on, get ready for bed. I'll climb in with you, and tell you a story. Sometimes stories make all the difference. How about 'Little Red Riding Hood'?"

"No, it's too scary. I feel sorry for the wolf. Wolves don't act like that! Read me some more about that beaver, Sajo."

I pick up my well-worn copy of Grey Owl's story of the two beaver kittens and begin to read.

"Chapter two, 'Gitchie Mee-Gwon, the Big Feather. Up the broad, swift current of the Yellow Birch river, in the days before the eyes of a white man had ever looked on its cool, clear waters, there paddled one early September morning a lone Indian in a birch-bark canoe.'"

By the time I get to the end of the chapter, to where Negik, the otter–the bitter and deadly enemy of all the Beaver People–is on the warpath and the beavers, their water gone, will now be fighting for their lives, Teddy is asleep, his head slumped against my arm.

I carefully untangle myself, and walk toward the stove to stoke it up. Just then I hear another "crack!" against the outside wall. I dive onto my bed and pull the feather quilt over my head. I try to think about anything but who might want to throw things at the house. I think of good times: picking berries with Millie, and hot summer days spent down by the creek with Teddy, and I think about birthdays....

Teddy's sixth birthday is on September 30th. It's his first birthday without Mom, but he still wants a party. We celebrate by inviting Ernie and Pat over for some of the birthday cake I've baked. Teddy gets a model airplane from Bean-Trap, and they immediately start to build it on the kitchen table. Glue sticks to everything and I begin to doubt it will ever fly.

"This is just like the airplane that Midnight flies!" Teddy exclaims.

I flash him a "Be quiet!" look. The Smiths are bad news around Bean-Trap.

"Who?" Bean-Trap asks.

"Oh, just some pilots in Fort Nelson–Bud, Midnight, Cannonball," I say casually.

He lets it pass and I breathe a sigh of relief.

♦ ♦ ♦

Now that it's officially October, the men in

Weasel City shut down their mining operations and get ready for trapping season. The women have been picking berries over the summer, and the hunters have brought home meat to dry and store. Everyone has been working to cut the meat and lay it in strips to dry on smoke racks. They also stretch, scrape and tan hides. They're now ready to be cut and sewn into mukluks, moccasins, leggings, coats, hats, and mitts. Nothing is wasted.

Millie shows me how to cut and sew in exchange for English lessons. I bought some coloured beads and am making and decorating mitts for Bean-Trap and Teddy for Christmas. I hide the stuff under my bed, and work on it while they're out of the cabin.

So far, I've shown Millie how to identify and sound out letters of the alphabet, and I've taught her some English words to describe household items: dishes, table, chairs. She can now read twenty words, and Teddy can read short sentences. Millie has more trouble with numbers, but Teddy is teaching her with cards. I think it's more of a game than a lesson, but I guess he gets that from Bean-Trap.

Bean-Trap has given me money to buy a few things at the store. I've sewn some blue curtains and a matching tablecloth for the kitchen, and Teddy and I braided rags into rugs so our feet won't freeze when we climb out of bed on cold mornings.

We still don't know many people around here

because Bean-Trap thinks it's better that way. We watch men arriving by boat, or walking in from the hills, and going up to the trading post with their mining profits. There, they pay off last season's debt with summer's gold and get ready for winter trapping season.

But while they are in town, Bean-Trap's "gaff", the local name for his gambling place, attracts nearly all of them.

Last night we did something we've been told never to do; Teddy and I sneaked a peek inside the gaff. There was so much smoke swirling around from the men's pipes and cigars that we could hardly see their faces. The gas lamps lit up the tables covered with green cloth.

As we watched, Bean-Trap dealt a card, face up, to each player.

"That's called their 'hole card'," Teddy informed me.

Then he dealt each player a second card, face down. "They're playing Stud Poker," Teddy whispered.

"How do you know?"

"I'm smart."

"Too smart sometimes."

"Dad showed me," Teddy says importantly. "See? That guy in the brown hat must have the highest card. He's starting the bets."

"Okay, now, be quiet and watch!"

The next man laid a bet, and the next, until the brass pot sitting on the table in front of Bean-

Trap overflowed with chits. The men were each dealt face-up cards until each man held five cards in his hands, including the hole card.

Suddenly we heard a noise behind us. We just managed to duck into the bushes when Mr. Benton, the burly trading post manager, came striding up the path and burst through the door of the gaff.

"Look, Braden, you're going to have to shut down!" Mr. Benton snapped. "I've had complaints from the wives, and from some of the men who've lost big. If you don't cooperate I'll bring the police in here to settle it."

We heard a chair scrape and imagined Bean-Trap standing with his hands balled into fists. We were hiding back in the trees, but their words carried clearly through the open door and poorly chinked log walls.

"Is Dad going to hit somebody now?" Teddy whispered.

"He'd better keep control," I reply. "Mr. Benton is pretty important around here. Everybody needs him. And they don't need Bean-Trap."

"If they're having fun, why don't they *like* him?" Teddy asked.

"Come on. Let's get out of here." We snaked through the poplars, intending to take a back-trail home but stopped in our tracks when we heard Mr. Benton's voice a few feet inside the window to our left.

"...and I had to give three men 'jawbone' to

send them out on their lines," Mr. Benton said loudly.

"Jawbone" means Mr. Benton had to lend the men money for their supplies.

"It's not my fault," Bean-Trap said stubbornly. "I don't drag them in here."

A chair fell over. Mr. Benton's footsteps stomped across the floor and his voice lashed out. "You're not hearing me, Bean-Trap! I didn't come to argue, I just came to tell you this in plain English. If any more guys come into my place needing money to see their families through the winter, I'll chase you out of town myself. I mean it! And there's not a man here who'd stop me!

"Weasel City is home to some good families who are trying to keep going while a World War rages on! Some have already served overseas, some are looking after grandchildren while the children's fathers are serving our country–and here you are, emptying their pockets with your games! I will not have it!"

Mr. Benton's heavy boots stomped back across the floor, the door opened, and then slammed shut. He strode past us through the bush. Teddy and I hid in silence. One by one, we saw the men leave the gaff.

"It's hard to explain why no one likes Bean-Trap," I said. "They only seem to like him when they're winning. But there's not much we can do about it now anyway."

We went back and sat on a bench outside the

cabin. When Bean-Trap came down the path, Miki ran to meet him. She yelped as Bean-Trap kicked her out of the way. Miki turned on him and Bean-Trap muttered a curse. Then Miki high-tailed it toward Millie and Pete's cabin. Our babysitter had quit.

I took Teddy's hand and we walked behind the cabin to a wooded trail that led to a bend in the river. I knew Bean-Trap would be mad at us for straying, but I didn't want to go inside and face him right then.

Teddy and I sat quietly on a rock and watched the sluggish flow of the dark river. "Snow's coming soon," I said, hugging my sweater around my shoulders.

"I know," Teddy said impatiently. "I'm cold, Loretta. Can't we go home?"

"In a little while. Let him cool off first."

"*I'm* cooling off!" Teddy said, as he started to shiver.

"Well, let's visit Millie instead then."

We followed the path, then cut through aspen trees nearly stripped of their autumn leaves, to Millie and Pete's cabin. I knocked on the door. The talking inside suddenly stopped. I knocked again and called out, "Hallo the house! It's Loretta and Teddy!"

Pat cautiously opened the door.

"We can't see you," he said bluntly.

Millie came up behind him and said something in Sikanni. Pat stepped back to let us in. I shoved

Teddy through the door and walked into their warm, homey cabin. But something felt different.

The four boys, Ben, Ernie, Pat and Harold, and the two girls, Louise and Alice, were sitting around the table, but the family wasn't eating. Tea wasn't offered. It looked like a meeting had been called, and we'd interrupted.

"Come," Millie said, indicating that Teddy and I were to sit down. "We need to talk."

"What's the matter?" Teddy asked Pat.

"You should know. It's your dumb Dad that's the problem!" Pat answered, but his mother and the others turned on him, "Sshhh!"

Millie gestured to the oldest boy, Ben, to talk, as he had the best English. He wouldn't look at either Teddy or me while he was speaking.

"Your Dad is bad," he mumbled. "He tries to take our money. You teach my mother to gamble." He stopped, and I realized it was as hard for him to say this as it was for me to hear it. I grabbed Teddy's hand under the table. He shook free, and stood up.

"That's a lie," he shouted. "Come on, Loretta. Let's go home."

I couldn't look at Millie. Miki came up, nuzzled my hand, then retreated under the table. No one tried to stop us as we headed for the door.

Outside, fine snow was starting to come down and a strong wind sent flurries into our faces. We were in for our first blizzard of the season.

Bean-Trap was nowhere to be found when we

got back to the cabin. I stoked up the stove and put on the kettle to make tea. "Maybe I'll make some raisin cookies," I said, and Teddy's face lit up.

We passed the rest of the evening eating and reading. I was halfway through a mouse-chewed Western novel. Teddy, for the umpteenth time, read the story of Jonah.

I know it's only a matter of time until people here decide to shove us overboard, but who will save us when *we* slide down the throat of a whale?

During November it snows almost every day. Most of the men have left the settlement to check their traplines, and Bean-Trap is getting restless. He knows they'll come back at Christmas with heaps of furs, and then there will be parties and lots of money to throw around.

Mr. Benton told me that the Alaska Highway is nearly completed, stretching fifteen hundred miles from Mile Zero at Dawson Creek B.C. to our old home of Fairbanks, Alaska. "Those big Caterpillars working from the north and the south will meet any day now!" he said.

Jay Smith and his family have been working on the highway, somewhere around the Liard River. He doesn't write very often. I've only had two letters from him since I met him in June. Both Teddy and I write to Bugs, too. He sent Teddy a domino set and a hair comb made with dyed porcupine quills for me. I keep them hidden from Bean-Trap. Mr. Benton gives me the letters personally; he seems to understand that Bean-Trap doesn't need to know everything. I keep them in my treasure box and re-read them until the paper shreds in my fingers.

I have Jay's last letter, dated July 16, almost memorized:

I am at our sawmill camp on the Liard River just a few miles away from where the new highway is going through. Dad and I bought partnerships in this mill, so maybe we'll get rich!

I think of you and your brother often. Write when you can steal a moment.

P.S. Bugs' letters are enclosed with mine–to save on stamps! He is studying to be a magician. Maybe he can make you appear here!

Teddy and I both like Bugs. He's eighteen, has lots of freckles and enjoys a good joke. He'd worked in a bank in Edmonton before deciding to head North for a bit more excitement. We're "North," but it doesn't seem so adventurous to me.

♦ ♦ ♦

Today Teddy and I are learning about the Sikanni people. Millie told me their story and I wrote a lesson.

"Sikanni means 'People of the Rocks' because they lived in the mountains," I begin, and Teddy says, impatiently, "I know! Ernie told me."

"They are of the Athapaskan group," I continue,

ignoring his fidgeting. "Long ago the Sikannis lived in pole lodges covered with spruce bark. In the summertime, the men wore laced sleeveless shirts and leather leggings made from animal skins. They used porcupine quills to decorate their clothes and wore bear-claw necklaces."

"I know. Ernie's dad has one. He showed me. He said the bear is his guardian spirit."

"Really?" I put down my notes.

"A few years ago, he was sent out into the bush alone. He didn't eat for four days. He dreamed of a bear. Now that bear looks after him. Ben and Ernie will have guardian spirits, too. Maybe even the wind or thunder."

"Do girls get guardian spirits, too?"

Teddy wrinkled his nose. "I think so. They can also can be healers, medicine people. Ernie's grandma is one."

The people here might be different than we are, but we share the same land, and the same hopes. "I wish Millie and her family could still visit us," I say quietly, remembering her stroking my hair.

"Yeah," Teddy agrees. "It's boring with no one to talk to but you."

"Okay, smarty, let's draw. That way, no one has to talk." Teddy decides to draw a bull moose wading into a swamp to eat some juicy plants. "Moose have big lips and broad teeth for browsing," I say, noting the pointed teeth he's drawing. "They don't graze as much as deer, and certainly don't have fangs like a wolf!"

Teddy ignores me and continues with his sketch, to be filled in with water paints later. I stroll around our cabin looking at the curtains, tablecloth and rag rugs which have given it a cozy look. The old stove has holes in its sides, but it still works, and we've never been cold. I wonder how our place would look to Jay.

I jump at a knock on the door. We haven't had any visitors for a long time. Teddy stops painting, his brush held in mid-air. We look at each other. I tip toe to the door.

"Who's there?" I say in my best grown-up voice.

I can barely hear the voice from the other side. "Millie."

I fling open the door. She stands looking down at her feet. "Come in!" I say with a huge smile.

She edges inside and I close the door against the blast of wind.

"Come in, take off your coat. I'll make tea!"

She hands me a small can of jam, like a peace offering, then shrugs out of her parka and removes her snowy mukluks.

"Hi!" Teddy says, happy for the diversion.

"A moose!" She says picking up his drawing. "It's good. He is two years old."

"How do you know?" Teddy asks.

"Long straight horns. Next year, they will be wide." She spreads the palms of her hands to show us the width of the horns the bull moose will have in his third year.

I set out the teapot, cups, and cookies. Before

I can pour our tea, Millie says, "Your Dad–he is okay. We are sorry. He didn't let Pete play cards. He didn't take his money." Her face turns even redder. "I told them, the cards are for me to learn numbers. That man, he told lie. He is bad man."

"Can I play with Ernie and Pat now?" Teddy asks, and Millie nods. "Yippee!" Before I can stop him Teddy has pulled on his parka and mukluks, and is out the door. Millie and I settle back to enjoy our tea, and the first real talk I've had in nearly two months.

♦ ♦ ♦

Some of the trappers start drifting into the settlements a few days later. They'd had good fall catches and decided to pull their traps and come home well before Christmas. Bean-Trap is delighted. In the mornings before he goes to work, he sings songs from Ireland about Paddy's Pig and Mrs. Murphy's Chowder. He plays cards with us by the hour, teaching us new games. He also shows us how to prepare a "cold deck" so that not even an expert would notice the exchange of a specially-stacked deck for the deck that had been shuffled in front of the players.

♦ ♦ ♦

Trouble surfaced the first week in December. When Black Mike Michaluk came snowshoeing down the river, carrying a bag of gold and a mysterious bundle of American money, everyone knew something was going to happen. Black Mike Michaluk didn't tell anyone where he'd got his money, and no one asked.

"Mr. High-and-Mighty Benton better keep his mouth shut," Bean-Trap said one day, just after Black Mike had arrived. "If he squeals to the Mounties about Mike carrying a 'bomb,' he'll be sorry. Real sorry."

"A bomb! He's got a bomb? Like in wars?" Teddy asks anxiously.

"No, a 'bomb' is cash. Money. *Lots* of money."

"Oh."

"But there *is* something funny about that guy. He's no 'apple'.

I knew that "apple" in Bean-Trap's language meant "sucker." Black Mike wasn't the kind of man who'd give up his money easily in a card game or some other scam. Black Mike was tough, a mysterious man with dark secrets.

"He's likely chilled someone off," Bean-Trap said. "I ain't trying any gimmicks on him. Guy like that, he'd shoot me between the eyes and leave me out for wolf bait."

Bean-Trap is good to us, but I can't deny that he's dangerous. Some say he's bad, and that he may be found dead some night with a 'shiv'–a long thin knife, like the one he carries in his boot–stuck into his ribs. In Weasel City, word of danger travels fast.

On December 3rd, Teddy came down with the flu. His face was flushed, he had a temperature, and his eyes were glazed. I filled a tub with cool water for his bath and Millie gave him some herbal medicine, which brought the fever down a bit.

Teddy wants Bean-Trap to stay home with him. Bean-Trap looks kind of helpless sitting there, but seems determined to do the right thing.

"Tell me a story," Teddy murmurs.

Bean-Trap scratches his head. His hair has grown longer than usual and is quite shaggy, as is his beard and scraggly mustache. "I got business pressures," he'd said gruffly when I mentioned his appearance. "I don't have time to think about my looks." But I know his real problem is Black Mike Michaluk.

"A story," Teddy repeats.

"Okay. I know one. It seems...."

"No! You have to say 'Once upon a time!'"

"Oh, okay." Bean-Trap clears his throat and

starts again. "Once upon a time there lived a famous casino card player, a Greek man named Nico Zographos. He was the boss of the Greek Syndicate, a huge organization that operated famous casinos in France, at Cannes and Deauville.

"Nico specialized in a game called baccarat, where the bank is auctioned off among the players. Highest bidder takes all. His bid sets the amount the other players bet against."

Teddy nods, quick to catch on.

Bean-Trap begins pacing the floor, swinging his great arms for emphasis. "So, one night at the casino in Deauville, Nico stands up and cries, 'Tout va!' This means there are no limits–his syndicate will cover any bet that a player wants to make."

"Were they really rich?"

"Really rich. But he's taking a big, big risk– the syndicate's money could all be lost on this one game–a game with the biggest and best gamblers in the world around the table."

"That's brave!" Teddy says.

"Brave, yes, but Nico's also smart! And he's an expert at baccarat. He can count faster than any man alive. Six packs–three hundred and twelve cards–are used in this game. They're dealt from a shoe, until less than nine cards are left. Then six more packs are shuffled, cut, and dumped into the shoe."

He leans toward Teddy, almost whispering, "Nico was so good, that when only nine cards were left he could name what they were. That means he could remember every card that had been played–over three hundred of 'em!"

Teddy's eyes are shining, from the fever and from excitement.

"Well, the great gamble worked, and hundreds of dollars changed hands. The syndicate cleaned up.

"They were honest men," Bean-Trap continues. "Their win was based on skill. They took one per-cent in profit and the rest went to the players."

"How much profit do you take?" I ask.

He ignores me.

"But one night, a few years later, Nico gets himself into real hot water. The syndicate has been losing for a long time, some said they were down to their last million francs. That's French money, and not very much. So, the big gamblers closed in for the kill, like a pack of wolves circling a moose stuck in a ten-foot snowbank.

"They force the syndicate to put up all its money on one game–everything could be lost with the turn of one card! When the cards were dealt the other players had good cards, but Nico–he drew the King of Hearts and the Queen of Spades–horrible! Nico got one more chance. He drew a third card, hoping it would improve his luck.

"No one around the table dared to breathe. Nico drew his card, and turned it over. The nine of diamonds!"

"The Curse of Scotland!" Teddy yelps.

"Right, son. Good boy. Well, it was the best

card old Nico could possibly have drawn. With that nine of diamonds, he won the game, and the syndicate's fortune was saved. After that, the nine of diamonds became his good-luck charm. He put it on everything–dishes, cuff-links, even on the flag he flew from his boat. With that nine of diamonds, the Greek Syndicate was out of danger, and on its way to fame and fortune."

"Are those men still playing?"

"You bet. An old gambler never dies–he just throws in his chips," he laughs.

I can't help but notice that Bean-Trap's big gold-rimmed teeth are stained yellow from the plug tobacco he buys now, instead of expensive cigars. He refuses to clean his teeth with baking soda and salt, like Mom taught us to do. I know he hadn't been having the good luck Nico did; his nine of diamonds was still out there, but how could we know when it would turn up?

♦ ♦ ♦

Early the next morning I awake to a knock at the door. Bean-Trap is still sleeping so I answer it.

A man dressed in tanned moosehide from head to foot stands in the doorway: a jacket decorated with beadwork and long fringes on the arms and across the chest, breeches, high wrap-around mukluks, and gauntlet-type mitts that reach almost to his elbows. I can tell he was not from around here. He has ice-blue eyes the colour of a Husky dog's, wild black hair, and a black beard. He is tall and strong, and obviously surprised to see me. He turns as if to leave, but then changes his mind and speaks, with a strange-sounding accent.

"Missy, I'm looking for your fadder."

I turn to glance back into the cabin, and nearly jump out of my skin. Dad is sitting up in bed with his revolver pointed at the door–and me. I dart to one side, leaving the stranger in firing range. Quick as a flash, the stranger removes a mitt and draws a gun.

I scream.

"Get away from here!" Bean-Trap yells. The stranger nods to me and backs down the path, his gun still pointed. When he has receded into the trees, I reach over and kick the door shut. My heart is pounding and I can't speak. Dad still sits up in bed, his revolver resting on the covers between his knees.

"I told them never to come to the house!" he says. "Especially that one."

"Black Mike Michaluk," I say, certain he was the famed bandit.

Teddy sits up, rubbing his eyes.

"Black Mike was here, and I was sleeping!" he says, peeved that he missed the action. "I wanted to meet him," he pouts. It is obvious he is over his fever.

Bean-Trap flings back his covers and strides over to Teddy's bed, still holding his gun. He's wearing the same set of long underwear he's had forever. "You don't ever want to meet people like him!" he barks at Teddy, who cowers under the covers. Bean-Trap looks at his hand, realizes he's packing the gun, and lays it on the table. "Sorry, kids. That won't happen again."

He slumps down onto a wooden chair. I look over at the table, and suddenly I bite my lip. I'd been looking in my treasure box earlier that morning, re-reading Jay's letters. His last one is lying in full view. I feel a wave of nausea as Bean-Trap picks it up. He leans forward, squints, and begins silently mouthing the words. When he turns to look at me, his face is red with fury.

"Smith! You're writing to that no-good Smith?"

"I did. Once," I say defiantly.

"Oh, you did, once! Well, ain't that nice. So even after I tell you it was his old man burned me out in Eagle, you still write and let them know where I am!" Dad rises so quickly that his chair falls over backwards. "Well, I got something to say to you!" He takes Jay's letter and rips it once, twice, then again and again until no piece is larger than a postage stamp. "If Jed Smith sends the cops out here after me, you, little lady, can take full blame!"

That does it. "You can't blame me for your problems! You are always in trouble, and it's nothing to do with me, or Jay Smith. You're in trouble right now with Black Mike Michaluk!"

He leaps toward me, grabs the collar of my

dress, and jerks me up until I'm swaying on my tiptoes. I stare at him straight in the eye and our gazes lock for several seconds. He lets me go.

"What's the use," he says. "I try to do good, raise my kids the only way I know how. Nothing works out. There's no use in a fellow like me trying to go straight."

Teddy is sobbing and I feel awful. "It's okay, anyway," I say. "Jay is moving to a sawmill in the middle of nowhere, somewhere way up the Alaska highway. I can't write him anymore."

"Don't matter. We're blowing out of here soon. Going south, into the Slocan Valley area, southern B.C. I hear there's dough there, lots of miners. Lots of gold yet in the hills. Get ready. Maybe we'll leave tonight, or tomorrow night. Trouble's coming, and when it does this place is gonna blow sky-high."

He gets up, quickly dresses, and leaves without washing or eating. I have a strange feeling in the pit of my stomach. There'll be a showdown at "the gaff." I'm sure of it.

♦ ♦ ♦

In the afternoon, Ernie and Pat ask Teddy to go outside and play. Millie's little girls have the flu, so we can't visit in case we get it. I clean up the cabin, bake a cake, and while it's cooling, decide to go to the trading post to buy some supplies.

Mr. Benton is talking to a group of men, and no one sees me enter. I am standing behind a row of high shelves looking at bolts of cloth when I hear the men mention the names Black Mike and Bean-Trap. I stay quiet to listen.

"...met his match...both scoundrels."

"Yeah, wouldn't doubt they knew each other up in Alaska or somewhere. Those kind band together."

"...either partners in some crooked business, or they'll kill each other over who gets what," one man snorts. "Black Mike's loot came from bad business–worse even than Bean-Trap's. At least we know where Bean-Trap gets his money!"

"Yeah...from us!" another man says. "Hey, Benton, you seen the colour of Black Mike's dough?"

"Yeah, I saw it," Mr. Benton replies. "And I'm not saying a thing about it. A man lives longer that way."

"You thinking what I'm thinking?"

There's a long silence.

"Of course. The American transport plane that went down last February out in the Tuchodi Lakes region. Right?"

"Funny no one's ever spotted it. Supposed to be loaded with payroll–American money–and pure gold." The man's tone becomes sly. "I recall seeing some of that here lately. Wonder what the police would say if American currency showed up in Weasel City?"

I don't even breathe. Bean-Trap's money, the money I watch him count each night when he comes home from "the gaff," has lately included gold and American money!

"Wonder how many men he had to finish off to rob the downed plane?"

"Oh, come on!" Mr. Benton slaps something onto the counter; the sound makes me jump. His voice has an angry tone. "So a plane crashed into a mountain. That happens often around here, especially with American pilots inexperienced in northern flying. Likely everyone on board was killed on impact. You can't say just because a prospector shows up with a bag of foreign coin, he's knocked someone off.

"Let's say you come across an American air force transport plane–a C-49–crashed on the side of a mountain, eighty miles south-southwest of Fort Nelson. There in the snow lies the payroll, half a million bucks in leather pouches, and gold, shining in the sun just like it fell from heaven.

"Now, you can't do a thing for these men. Someone will find them sooner or later, and take their i.d. to the Air Force so their families can be told–but who'll get the money? The United States government, that's who! Any of you boys have a particular allegiance to Uncle Sam?"

Mr. Benton pauses to look around.

"The money's there, and the gold, just like you find it lying in riverbeds, only this time it's in leather bags, ready to go," he continues. "So, let's say Black Mike stumbles on the wreckage, picks up the coin, comes into Weasel City, drops a bit in Bean-Trap's gambling joint, a bit more here outfitting himself for next year's mining. Can't hang a man for that!"

The men mutter, and I hear them shuffle out, one by one. I wait a few minutes, then emerge from my hiding place.

"Well! How long have you been there?" Mr. Benton asks.

"I just came in," I mutter. Mr. Benton's eyes crinkle slightly. He knows I'm lying, but he's going to let me get away with it. That's the code of the North–hear nothing, see nothing, say nothing. You learn that early on, and as Mr. Benton said, you live longer that way.

I buy some thread and a box of baking soda, put it on Bean-Trap's bill, and head for home. I can't get what I've overheard out of my mind. Did Black Mike really find a wrecked plane and rob it? Were the people all dead? Some of the money Bean-Trap has won from Black Mike is cached under our floor. Dead men's–maybe murdered men's–money.

I see Millie standing in the doorway of her cabin. "I won't come in, I know the kids are sick," I say, "but...." Suddenly I don't know what to say so I run down the path. I hear her call, "Good-bye!" and turn and give a quick farewell wave. Her hair is neatly done in a coiled braid, and she's wearing an apron over a blue-flowered dress. Later, I remember her that way.

Back at the cabin, I put more wood on the fire and try not to think about leaving Weasel City.

When Teddy returns, I run to the door and hug him hard. He squawks, and I laugh at myself for getting so spooked.

After supper, Teddy and I read stories, but neither of us wants to hear the scary ones. I take out the Bible and start reading from Genesis, but I soon realize I've made a bad choice. Abraham is told by God to sacrifice his son.

"Take your son," God says, "your only son, Isaac, whom you love so much, and go to the land of Moriah. There on a mountain, offer him as a sacrifice to me."

I think of other peoples' sons sacrificed on a mountain not far from here, and the gold that rests in a canvas bag under the floorboards beneath our feet.

Teddy soon tires and goes to bed. I can't sleep so I sit up late with the lamp turned down low just thinking. I can't read in the poor light and I've already read everything here anyway and I can't write in my journal because Bean-Trap might discover it and cause trouble.

All I can do is think. I think of Jay and Bugs and wish they were here to cheer me up and tell me stories of Jay's famous uncle, a pilot named Midnight Smith. I decide to write Jay and hope that Bean-Trap won't find the letter before I can mail it. As I write, I know it will be the last letter

I'll ever send from Weasel City.

Dear Jay:

We're moving, very soon. Bean-Trap found your letter and got really mad. I told him you'd moved and were somewhere up the Alaska highway but he tore up your letter and forbade me to write you anymore. We might be moving south to stay ahead of the trouble that seems to follow Bean-Trap wherever we go. I'll try to write again when we get settled.

Your friend, Loretta.

I seal the envelope, hide it inside my coat pocket, and plan to take it to the trading post tomorrow.

I fall asleep imagining Jay and I–and Teddy– flying over the mountains in his uncle's plane. Suddenly, we crash against a rocky cliff and the plane bursts into flames, pieces of metal shooting into the sky. I'm lying on the ground, someone is kicking me, reaching into my pockets, stealing my letters.

I wake up, sweating, breathing in gasps. Before I can figure out if I'm awake, the door flies open and Bean-Trap rushes in.

"Quick! Get up, Loretta! We have to pack! Wake Teddy! We're leaving! NOW!"

We have one hour to get everything together: clothes, food, blankets, matches, guns and ammunition, a small first-aid kit and emergency supplies including a fifty-pound test line that can be used for sewing anything from wounds to torn clothing. I grab my treasure box and shove it deep into a bag.

We'll be going out on a sled pulled by a single file dog-team, travelling by moonlight. We need to get to Dawson Creek, nearly four hundred miles away and from there, we'll take a train to Edmonton.

Bean-Trap rasps out instructions. "Hurry! Just two bags–grub in one, clothes in another. Blankets in the carry-all! Move quickly!"

He yanks back the floorboards and takes out his cache of money and gold, fastening the canvas bags onto a special belt around his waist. I notice blood seeping through his shirt. "You're hurt!" I cry, but he quickly buttons his parka to disguise the bags and his injury. We drag our baggage out the door, take it around the side of the cabin where a Cree Indian man waits, his dogs muzzled quiet as the snow. As we close the door to our cabin I see our little stove still glowing with the last log.

Silently, Teddy and I climb into the carry-all, while Bean-Trap and the driver prepare to run behind. I turn to get a last glimpse, but snow is falling and in less than a minute our home, Millie's cabin, Mr. Benton's trading post, and everything else in the little settlement of Weasel City fades to white.

We head down to the river to travel on the ice. When we're a few miles out, Bean-Trap begins to stagger. The Cree man stops the team so that Bean-Trap can sit down on an outcropping of ice at the river's edge. He's panting, and his face gleams with sweat in the moonlight. He and the man talk rapidly in Cree.

Teddy is sobbing, and I'm so scared my teeth are chattering. I get our home medicine kit from the bag, and open a tin of medicated ointment. I hand it to Bean-Trap who swabs it over his wound, still shielding it from sight.

The man takes a shirt from one of the bags, rips it into strips, and ties it tightly around Bean-Trap's big middle, padding a pair of clean socks over the wound. There's nothing more we can do on the trail.

I know, without having to be told, that we're still

in danger. We must put as many miles between us and Weasel City as we can before daylight.

The dogs jump ahead, jerking the sled as we bump down the snow-covered river ice–the northern highway that is our only hope for escape.

I must have fallen asleep, because when I awaken a rim of light lines the eastern horizon. The dogs are trotting at a pace they've kept for hours. We pull over to the riverbank, and the man says something to Bean-Trap in Cree.

"Go get some kindling, we're making a fire and cooking some grub. Take a trip into the bushes if you need to. We aren't stopping long." Bean-Trap is gasping, and his face is very pale.

Teddy and I get stiffly out of the carry-all and stumble toward a thin patch of willows. I feel miserable–my stomach is churning and I wonder if I am coming down with the flu. But I can't! We have three hundred and fifty miles to go.

"Where are we going Dad?" Teddy rubs his eyes and yawns, looking around at the grey sky and snow-covered hills.

"The first town is Fort Nelson. Guess I'll have to see a doc. Then, south. Stop in Edmonton–got some business there–then take the train, bus, whatever, across the border at Sweetgrass, Montana to Butte."

"Why Butte?"

Bean-Trap gets an excited look on his face that overcomes his pain. "The city of Butte is a mile high and a mile deep! It's got copper and

SHIRLEE SMITH MATHESON

zinc mines and plenty of opportunities."

"But you're not a copper miner," I say. "You mine gold!"

He grins weakly, and his gold-rimmed teeth flash. "That's right. They go underground–I stay above ground and mine gold!"

"What about the Slocan Valley? You said we might go there."

"Shhh! We're going to muddy up our trail. We'll get across the border, go down to Butte, find out what's going on, then go west to Spokane and quietly sneak back into Canada–same way most Yankees got into that rich mining country." He laughs, which comes out a painful bark, and the Cree man jumps. He isn't used to Bean-Trap's brusque manner, but we are. Nobody can quiet him when he's on the trail of gold.

The Cree man, who we're told is named Val, talks only to Bean-Trap and his dogs. It's as if Teddy and I don't exist. When we get to Fort Nelson we wait down by the river while Bean-Trap finds a doctor. He is back that afternoon looking a lot better.

"Just a nick." He laughs, throwing something over to me. I reach out to catch it before I realize what it is. In my hand nestles a blood-encrusted bullet.

"Wow!" says Teddy.

I lean over a snowbank, and throw up.

♦ ♦ ♦

We have followed the Muskwa River from Weasel City to Fort Nelson. Now we travel the Nelson River to Mile 278, overland to Fontas at the back of Trutch, hit the Sikanni Chief River on the other side of Trutch, and then follow a pack trail and the Beatton River to Fort St. John.

We could have travelled on the new Alaska Highway part of the way, but it's already busy with army vehicles and we're afraid of being discovered. We pass by Fort St. John, cross over the Peace River, and finally reach Dawson Creek.

Bean-Trap pays Val and says good-bye. Without a word or a backward glance, he turns his dogs and sled and heads north, likely glad to be rid of us.

Teddy has never seen a train before and he is wild with excitement. A man at the station explains that this was once the Edmonton, Dunvegan and British Columbia Railway, but is now part of the Northern Alberta Railway system. It runs from Dawson Creek, B.C. into Alberta, through Hythe and Grande Prairie, and southeast to Edmonton. It is mostly used to haul freight, but some American Pullman coaches have been added to transport the Americans coming up to work on the highway.

I can't believe how elegant everything is! The seats are plush, and the dining cars, which belong to the N.A.R., are fabulous! The waiters wear crisp white jackets and the tables are draped with white cloths and set with beautiful china and sparkling silverware. I suddenly feel very shabby.

There are lots of soldiers on board and some smile at us. Bean-Trap wants to get the latest war news. I try to follow, but it sounds very mixed up: Allied forces are in North Africa, British troops have captured Tobruk, Russians counter-attacked at Stalingrad...and the Japanese are still threatening to sneak into Alaska from the Aleutian Islands!

During our train ride to Edmonton, I finally have a chance to talk to Bean-Trap in private and ask the one question that has been burning in my mind ever since he stormed through our door.

"What happened in Weasel City?"

"Nothing much. Bit of a dust-up."

"Black Mike?"

He looks around, as if afraid we're being spied on. "Look, Loretta, what you don't know won't hurt you. Leave the business end of this family to me, okay? Whatever happens, you and Teddy will be looked after. That's why we're stopping over in Edmonton. I'm leaving some money in a bank there, a lot of money, and I'm giving you the account number. You memorize it so if you ever need it, you'll know where to go."

"What's going to happen to you?"

"Nothing! But, I mean to look after you, even

if I ain't the best kind of father. You'll never have to 'toady' to anyone. You understand?"

I nod, although I don't understand at all. I think of Black Mike's ice-blue eyes, and his quick revolver. I knew it was his gun that shot the bullet lodged in Bean-Trap's side. Black Mike was no "apple."

We arrive in Edmonton December 24th–two days before my fifteenth birthday. Airplanes are flying to and from the Blatchford airfield every few minutes; bush planes, American air force transport planes and bombers, taking military supplies and people north to the bases along the Alaska Highway. People everywhere are talking about the war.

From the train station we take a cab to a fine hotel called The MacDonald, and get a big room with three beds. Bean-Trap hands Teddy and I some money. "Here, go out, buy some treats, get yourself a Christmas present if you like. I'll be back in a couple of hours."

"Where are you going, Dad?" Teddy asks.

"Have to see a man about some business." He winks at me, and indicates the roundness under his coat. "Gotta bank this 'bomb'. He flashes his gold teeth.

"Bugs works in a bank!" Teddy says, before I can shut him up.

"Who?"

"Just a fellow we met in Fort Nelson," I say hurriedly.

His eyes narrow. "Some friend of Jed Smith's? I don't want no banker in Edmonton reporting to no one back home where I'm at! So you better tell me."

"He's a friend of Jay's, not Jed's, and right now he's up at a sawmill somewhere on the Alaska Highway. He used to work in a bank in Edmonton," I explain. "He's not here anymore."

"Oh." Dad looks unconvinced, and I push Teddy in the ribs to shut him up.

"Well, you be back in two hours. Meet me right here," Bean-Trap says. "I guess banks are banks, safe as Fort Knox." He laughs and flips Teddy and I each a fifty-cent piece, to add to the money he's already given us.

"Be sure to see a doctor, too!" I call after him, but I don't think he heard me.

"What does he need a bank for?" Teddy asks as we stroll down Jasper Avenue. "Is he going to rob it?"

"No, no. Bean-Trap doesn't rob banks!" I say. Two ladies stare, and I realize I have spoken too loudly.

"You'd better stop calling him that," Teddy says. "You should call him Dad. We're starting over, remember?"

I nod absently. "Let's go to Eaton's. We can see all the things we used to look at in the catalogue."

Teddy laughs. "Does Eaton's know we used their catalogues in the outhouse, after we'd sent in our orders?"

"Hey, I want to leave that part of bush-life behind, if you don't mind!" I laugh. I hoped we'd live in a big city like Edmonton and have indoor plumbing, electric lights, sidewalks, brightly-lit stores, and all the latest fashions.

Silver bells and streamers decorate the walls and high ceilings of Eaton's main floor. A big Christmas tree nearly reaches the roof. Christmas carols are playing on a phonograph.

I can smell a beautiful scent that Grandma called lavender. It reminds me it will be our first Christmas without Mom. I suddenly miss her so much I almost burst into tears. Stifling them, we walk up to the second floor so Teddy can see the toys.

"Oh, Loretta, is it really Santa Claus?" Teddy whispers, pointing in the direction of his big chair.

"Yes, I'm sure it is. Let's just wait here."

Santa Claus looks over at us and smiles. His bright blue eyes twinkle. "Hello, children!" he calls. "Come and see old Santa." I push Teddy forward. Santa holds out his hand and pulls Teddy onto his lap. "What's your name, son?"

"Teddy."

"Well, Teddy, have you been a good boy?"

Teddy looks puzzled. "I think so," he says slowly, as if he's never thought about it before.

"Good! So what would you like for Christmas this year? What can old Santa bring you?"

Teddy purses his lips in deep thought. "I'd like

Mom to come back," he says softly. "She died last year, but I want her to come back so we can all be together again."

"Well, Teddy, Santa will do what he can to help you," he says. His voice sounds kind of choked.

He gives Teddy and I a bag of candy and I thank him. He puts a "BACK IN 10 MINUTES" sign on the stage and takes off.

"You stay here while I go look at dresses," I say when we're in the toy section, but Teddy doesn't hear me. He is captivated by a train that chugs on a little figure-eight-shaped track, through tunnels and over bridges, blowing its whistle at every curve.

I quickly pass through the "Children's Wear" department to an area called "Young Ladies' Fashions." I stand and stare at baby-blue, soft pink, and mint-green silky dresses, shiny black patent-leather shoes, stockings so sheer I can see through them, blouses with lace collars, sweaters with roses knit into their patterns, hair ribbons and barrettes of every colour. I feel in my pocket for the money Bean-Trap gave me.

"May I help you?" a lady asks.

I look over at the display of hair ribbons. "How much?" I ask, pointing to a cascade of brightly-coloured ribbons.

"Five cents a foot," she says. "And the barrettes match. They are twenty-five cents a pair."

"I'll take that pair of red barrettes, and three

feet of the narrow red ribbon," I say quickly. "Oh, and some green ribbon too, for Christmas."

I wander back to Teddy, who hasn't moved an inch from the train display. "How much for the little train set?" I ask.

"Six ninety-five without the tunnels or signs, nine ninety-five with everything. That includes the engine, the Pullman car, the caboose and track."

"I'll take the full set!" I announce. Teddy's mouth is hanging open as he watches the clerk wrap his Christmas gift.

"I'm sorry that it won't be a surprise on Christmas morning," I say, "but I think it's extra nice to get something you really want, don't you?"

For once in his life, Teddy is speechless. I offer to carry the box, which is fairly large, but he insists on doing it himself even though he can barely wrap his arms around it.

"One more stop before we go back to the hotel." I go over to the counter that sells men's ties.

"For Dad?" Teddy says, his eyes wide. "He doesn't wear ties!"

"He will. You just watch!" I select two nice ties, a red one and a green one. "We're city folk now!"

On Christmas morning I give Bean-Trap and Teddy the decorated moosehide mitts I've made for them. "Wow!" Teddy and Bean-Trap say in unison. The wonderful smell of the tanned mitts makes us all homesick. But not for long.

Bean-Trap produces a wool cap and mitts for Teddy, and a small silver locket for me. I look at him and, for the first time in my life I say, "Thanks...Dad."

I won't ever take it off. I wish I had a picture to put inside.

Teddy and I give him his ties. A big smile comes over his face. "These are great!" he says. "You bet I'll wear them! I want to look real spiffy when I start working again."

"Are you going to have another gaff in the Slocan Valley?"

Bean-Trap's face takes on a secretive look. "Maybe. After things cool off a bit."

"What things?"

He is obviously trying to decide how much he should tell us. Finally he says, "I don't want undesirable people to follow us. That's why we're dipping south of the old '49th parallel and coming back into Canada through the pass. Don't worry–we've got enough money to tide us over until spring.

"Now, Loretta, you look gorgeous with your new locket, and those red ribbons and barrettes. But why didn't you buy a new dress and shoes to go with them? For your birthday."

I smile, and decide to let him get away with his obvious attempt to change the subject.

"Both of you should get new outfits for school."

"We'll be going to a real school!" Teddy's eyes are shining, and I guess mine are too. This new life sounds more exciting every day.

◆　◆　◆

We board another train, a Canadian Pacific Railway branch line, to go from Edmonton to Calgary, then another train to Lethbridge. We take a bus from Lethbridge to cross the border at Coutts on the Alberta side, and Sweetgrass on the Montana side.

Now that Teddy owns a train, he says he's going to be a conductor. He nearly talks the ears off the conductors on our train, who are forced to look at, and admire, his new Christmas present.

Personally, I'm glad he is considering a career other than his father's. I'll buy some train books so I can tell him a train story for every one of Bean-Trap's gambling stories!

As we near the border, Bean-Trap becomes quiet and looks uneasy. A man in uniform boards the bus.

"Ears and eyes open, mouths shut!" Bean Trap suddenly barks to us.

As the border inspectors proceed down the aisle of the bus, I see a film of sweat form on Bean-Trap's forehead. He wipes it with his hand-kerchief. The inspectors are checking everyone. I hear them ask people what their names are, where they were born, where they're going, and how long they're staying. They come to us.

"Name, sir!"

"William Jonathan Benedictson and these are my children, Loretta and Teddy–ahh, Theodore – Benedictson." The man doesn't seem to notice our shocked looks when he gives these names.

"Do you have their birth certificates?"

"I've got 'em."

He *does*? I've never seen my birth certificate. And how did he get Teddy's and his own made out in my last name?

Bean-Trap reaches inside his suit jacket, pulls out a leather folder, and hands the man some papers.

He looks at the documents. "Thank you, sir," the inspector says. "You and your children have permission to enter the United States of America."

When the bus is moving again, I ask, "How did you get those certificates? My real name is Benedictson, but yours, and Teddy's, is Braden...."

"Sshh! Don't say that name, ever again! From now on we're the Benedictsons, got it?"

Teddy and I nod obediently.

"I got some paperwork done in Edmonton," he says in a low voice. "I knew it would come in handy. Didn't realize how soon."

I turn to look out the window, not wanting Teddy to see my confused expression.

♦   ♦   ♦

Montana is beautiful! At first we see the snow-covered flats, but then mountains and valleys appear as we follow along the Missouri River.

We stay overnight at Helena, the capital of Montana. The next day we walk past a museum and at our insistence, and because it's my birth-day, Bean-Trap takes us inside.

We find out that the name Montana comes from a Spanish word meaning 'mountainous'. The early settlers called this 'The Land of Shining Mountains'. Bean-Trap gets interested only when he learns that the mountains running through here and up into British Columbia contain vast amounts of gold and silver.

"See, I told you we were coming to the right

place!"

"The main street here is called Last Chance Gulch!" I inform him.

"Gold–right in the streets!" Bean-Trap says, and twirls his mustache. He looks much better since he got a haircut and his beard and mustache trimmed in Edmonton.

He buys us souvenirs and treats us to a dinner in the fanciest hotel in Helena. "Happy birthday, Loretta," he says at dinner and hands me a little package. Inside is a pair of gold earrings. "I gave these to your mother, now I'm giving them to you."

The earrings suddenly become blurry and I can't speak.

"And here's my present for you," Teddy says and shoves a package toward me. Inside is a small pen and paper set that he'd bought in the museum shop.

"They're wonderful presents. Thanks so much." I have a feeling that fifteen is going to be a good year.

♦ ♦ ♦

We travel on to Butte. It is warmer here than in Weasel City. We can walk down the street with our coats open, although Bean-Trap tells us not to.

"I don't want you getting sick on me," he says. "We've still got some travelling to do."

He leaves us in the hotel room while he goes out to check on the "business district." I know he's finding out where the money is, and keeping in mind future locations for gaffs if we have to come back this way.

He returns in high spirits. "This territory is booming!" he cries. "The war is the best thing that ever happened to the economy."

We take a train to Spokane, the connecting city between mining operations in Washington State and British Columbia. Hundreds of ore cars, both loaded and empty, pass us.

We stay in Spokane for two days while Bean-Trap gets the low-down on current action in B.C.'s Slocan, Lardeau and Kootenay districts.

We board another train north to Nelson and then on to Kaslo, B.C. I'm frightened when I see the train tracks have been built on rickety-looking wooden trestles that curve around mountain-sides miles above deep gorges. I feel sure we're going to fall off the rails and crash. Teddy finds the trip totally exciting.

"We could go west from Kaslo to the Slocan Valley like I'd planned and check out Three Forks and Sandon," Bean-Trap says, "but I don't like what I've heard about this area. The place is busy all right, but not with miners."

"So, who's there?" I ask.

"Since Japan attacked Pearl Harbour a year ago, the Japanese from the west coast have been moved inland and ended up in Sandon. They won't have any money to throw around and the police force will be there thick as fleas on a dog's back. We're going up country to Lardeau–take a look at Ferguson, Cambourne, Lardeau City, old gold mining areas in there. I hear that everyone's predicting another strike."

"Great! I want to live in a city."

Bean-Trap laughs. "Don't get your hopes up, Loretta. This 'city' won't be much different from Weasel City, but they both have just what I need for a while."

"What's that?" I ask.

"Miners, money–and no law enforcement."

♦ ♦ ♦

We arrive in Ferguson after dark on New Year's Eve, 1942. As the train pulls into town, we hear music coming from the hotels that line the main street. Bean-Trap can't get the grin off his face.

Bean-Trap informs the man at a fancy place called the Hotel Lardeau that we need a room for the night.

"There ain't any," he says.

"So where can I rent a room for me and my kids?"

The man shrugs. "All full," he says and turns away.

"Just one minute mister!" Bean-Trap leans across the counter and grabs the man by the arm. "I got two little kids here and they ain't sleepin' out on the street. You tell me where we can get a room."

The man stands back and brushes his arm as if Bean-Trap has left something dirty on his sleeve. "You can likely find something down the street at the Liberty. It ain't much; they cater mostly to miners, but it's clean."

"Thanks."

We pick up our heavy suitcases, which we'd bought in Edmonton to replace the canvas bags packed from the North, and go back onto the street. The Liberty isn't really a hotel, it's a doorway and stairs wedged in between two stores. We climb a steep wooden staircase. Each step creaks and the walls give off a smell of old, dry wood and dust. Even Teddy and I are puffing when we reach the top; Bean-Trap is positively wheezing.

There is a barred wicket in the side of the wall where an old woman sits. She looks like she just got out of bed. Her grey hair is in a long braid hanging down over one shoulder. She hasn't even put in her teeth.

"We need a room, my kids and me," Bean-Trap pants.

She shoves a book over to him. "Sign here. Buck a night. Let me know two hours before you pull out. What mine you workin'?"

Bean-Trap laughs. "Grandma, I ain't no miner–but someday you'll have a sign over this door that says, 'William J. Benedictson Stayed

Here.' You remember that! My name is going to be one of the most famous in this town."

"*Dobre,*" the woman says. "That means you'll leave this joint heading south, in the Premier's train car or trussed up in a straight-jacket with the RCMP prodding your butt. Or you might never leave–just find yourself stuffed into a pine box and buried under six feet of mined earth. That's the fate of the big names that come here. Read about 'em every day in the Ferguson *Eagle.*" She smiles at Teddy and me.

"When you get settled, you two come and see 'Grandma'. I just baked a few flats of ginger snaps and I was wonderin' what I was going to do with them all. My boys like my snaps, but they don't need 'em all. They're too fat already!"

She grins toothlessly, and I've never seen such a beautiful face in my life. I sure need a grandma, and from the sound of it I think I've found her already, right here in Ferguson.

We are given a big room containing cots, a dresser, and a wardrobe that smells of mothballs. Our windows face main street, which looks like the site of a high-noon showdown in a Wild West movie. Big, old false-fronted buildings (most have seen better days) line the street, some with lights on, some that look abandoned. People walk up and down the snowpacked street.

We watch men and women going in and out of the hotels. "Folks here must never go to bed," Teddy says. Every time a hotel door opens, we hear dance music and shouting. Above the town, snowy tree-covered mountains stand silently above it all.

♦ ♦ ♦

In the morning, we take turns using the bathroom at the end of the hall. Men come and go from their rooms, nod politely to us, and call out "Hello, Grandpa!" or "Good-bye, Grandma, see you next week!" to the two old people who run this place. Grandpa has a beard, long white hair combed straight back, and wears thick glasses. He is dressed in blue jeans, a plaid shirt, a black leather vest, and cowboy boots.

"Good morning, young 'uns! Grandma told me we had two kids staying here. You must be Loretta and Teddy!" he says, stopping us in the hallway.

"We heard music all night!" Teddy says.

Grandpa laughs. He takes out a pouch of tobacco and paper, and expertly rolls a cigarette.

Bean-Trap sees us talking to Grandpa and comes over. As soon as they meet eye to eye, they recognize each other.

"'Doc' Bond," Bean-Trap says softly. "So, you still gettin' away with it?"

"Looks like–till you came 'round, Bean-Trap. Didn't recognize you by your new moniker–Benedictson."

"Or me you. What name you hanging on yourself now, Rockerfeller?"

Grandpa laughs. "We may be usin' new names, but don't try pullin' no 'acky-lark' on an old fence! Woloshyn's the name. We run this place, me and the missus."

Bean-Trap and Grandpa eye each other for a moment and a look of understanding seems to pass between them.

"Now, where'd you kidnap these kids?" Grandpa says.

"He didn't kidnap us!" Teddy cries.

Both men laugh, but they are still poised like two foxes eyeing one another, neither willing to make the first move.

I speak up. "My father, my brother Teddy and I have come to live in Ferguson. We're going to find a nice place to rent, and then we'll start school."

"Honey, we'll do all we can to help you, but finding a place to rent in this town ain't no easy job. Everyone's come here to find work. There's nothing empty, not even a coal-shed." Grandpa looks at me, his big glasses making his eyes appear twice their real size.

Then he grins and winks. "Naw, you'll do fine. Go and see Grandma. She hears all the news, quicker than the newspaper. She'll find you a place nearby. School, eh? Me, I can't read too good, but that's never held me back none. Ain't that right, Bean-Trap?"

Bean-Trap's face flushes. "Right," he says.

"What's an 'acky-lark'?" Teddy whispers as we go back to our room.

"How should I know?" I snap.

"I'm getting tired of meeting people who have something against Dad." Teddy says. "What's he ever done?"

"I don't think we need to know."

But the minute Bean-Trap enters our room, I pounce. "Why'd you call Grandpa 'Doc'? What did he mean, don't pull no 'acky-lark with an old fence'? What's going on?"

He closes the door and walks to the window.

"Pay no attention to that kind of talk," he says gruffly, avoiding us. "It's just bits of old news."

"Come on!"

He turns to face us. "Okay. A 'fence' sells things that come his way, from, uh, various sources. He don't ask questions, but he's not going to be fooled about what he's buying. When he gets gold he tests it using nitric acid. It's called an 'acky' test, from the words *aqua-fortis*. Ah, you don't need to know all this stuff. You're just kids!"

"But I want to!" I insist. "I want to know things."

"Me too," Teddy adds.

He sighs and continues. "Okay. So if an 'acky' is a fence's test of gold, an 'acky-lark' is a trick some people use to substitute a straight solution for the aqua-fortis, so the gold will test true when it's not. Or, they can 'salt' the mines...."

"How?"

"Get a bag of cheap gold fragments, then just sprinkle gold bits into a rack of empty sample bags. The rock dust mixes with the gold dust. Or, you coat the samples with a liquid gold solution. It ain't hard."

"Everyone is cheating," I say.

He nods. "You're learning, Loretta."

"Why did you call Grandpa Woloshyn, 'Doc' Bond?" Teddy asks.

"It's a long story. He used to 'doctor' lots of things–certificates, bonds. But his specialty was using chemicals. That man could turn dirt into gold if he put his mind to it. He's a miner trained in chemistry, or a chemist trained in mining, something like that. A real smart duck." He sighs.

"I'm tired of hearing about people who cheat to get ahead," I say. "It doesn't get them anywhere. Look at Grandpa and Grandma, living here in this dirty old hotel! And look at us! We've got less than nothing!"

Bean-Trap's expression is sullen. I know I've hurt his feelings.

"People like Grandpa and me, we try to go straight, but it never works out."

"Maybe you should try again."

"Maybe so."

♦ ♦ ♦

We spend the morning with Grandma, who looks worse today than she did last night. Her hair is grey and nicotine-stained to match her fingers. Her long braid hangs over one shoulder, secured by a rubber band. She still hasn't put her teeth in. Her clothes are unmatched, like she's walked through the room picking up a green blouse here, a blue and white sweater there, and found an orange parachute which she's made into "balloon" pants. Her slippers turn up at the toes, and are made of red satin. She's not my real Grandma, but she sure is colourful!

The two-room apartment smells of fresh coffee and buns, mixed with a spicy aroma of yesterday's gingersnaps. In a box in the corner, a big fluffy grey cat is curled around a litter of kittens.

"Her name's Sapphire," Grandma says when Teddy and I kneel down to admire the kittens. "When you get settled, you can have one. They'll be ready to leave their mamma in a couple weeks. You should have your own place by then."

Teddy picks up a mottled grey kitten, but I immediately fall in love with one that Grandma says is a "tortoise-shell." Its fur is cream-coloured, with bright black and yellow patches.

"Can we have this one?" I ask. Grandma nods. I look at Teddy.

"It's okay–you can have him if Dad lets us keep one," Teddy concedes. "I'll be too busy playing with my new friends to have time for a cat."

I smile at him and gently put *my* kitten back into the box beside its mamma. "Thank you, Teddy. It will be our kitten, but I'll look after it when you get too busy. You can name it, if you like."

"Let's call it Angel."

"Got news for you," Grandpa announces, over-hearing my words. "Your Angel is a tom."

"Can't boys be angels too?" Teddy asks.

"Of course they can!" I say.

"Angel is a pretty special kitten," Grandma says. "You don't see male tortoise-shells every day. Maybe one in fifty thousand."

"Then he's valuable! We can take the other one."

"No, no! He's yours. Thing is, all male tortoise-shells are sterile."

"What does that mean?" Teddy asks.

"He can't father kittens," Grandma says quickly.

"Oh. Well, that's okay. One's enough."

"It looks like you got yourself a four-footed mouse trap!" Grandpa says. He winks at us behind his magnifying glasses.

♦ ♦ ♦

The next day, Grandma tells us she knows of a house for rent. "It belongs to one of my miners, but he's never there. It's not been kept up and there's sure to be mice in it. Angel is just what you need."

Grandpa offers to drive us over to the house in his old beat-up panel truck. The place isn't very fancy. The picket fence is unpainted and falling in. Two-foot high frozen weeds decorate the yard. Grandpa unlocks the door. Inside it's not so bad, just unlived-in. The furniture is enough to get by, and there are two bedrooms. It doesn't have electricity or running water, but an indoor toilet and a bath-tub that sits on four claw feet are set up in the bathroom.

It's a nicer place than the old one-room cabin in Weasel City, and the stove is in a lot better shape. But suddenly I get homesick for the little place on the bank of the Muskwa River, for Millie and Mr. Benton and the beautiful forest.

I know that the line of mountains outside Ferguson joins up to the ridge of the Rockies I saw from our cabin in Weasel City, but a thousand miles of rock stands between us.

"How much does the guy want for this shack?"

Grandpa mutters a figure, then adds, "Less than that, if you fix the place up a bit."

"That include your cut?" he asks. Grandpa smiles.

"Okay," Bean-Trap agrees, and just like that, it's ours.

"Where is the school from here?" I ask and Grandpa points down the winding road.

"Can we go there now?" Teddy asks.

"Don't see why not," Grandpa says. "You can get registered this afternoon. You're already four months late. You'll have lots of catchin' up to do."

♦ ♦ ♦

We pull up in front of a white building. "You can even get your high school diploma here, if you take some courses through the mail," Grandpa says.

Bean-Trap and Grandpa walk in with us. A man comes out of his office, then stops in his tracks, staring from Bean-Trap to Grandpa as if they looked like they might hold up a train!

I step up. "My brother and I want to register for school here."

"Oh, yes. Well, I'm Mr. Phipps, the principal." He coughs and turns to a woman who is sitting at a desk tapping on a big typewriter. "We have some new students here," he says as if she hasn't seen us. She hands him some papers for us to fill out. He coughs again. "Come into my office," he says.

Bean-Trap and Grandpa haven't said a word, but the secretary and two teachers who have gathered at the front desk are staring. We go in and close the door. The principal opens it again. "Nothing secret around here," he booms. "Everything out in the open!"

I can tell that he's scared of us, but I also know that he's an "apple."

"Now, what is this little man's name?" the principal asks, looking at Teddy.

"What's yours?" Teddy asks.

"Oh, yes. I am Mr. Phipps. Welcome to Silver Cup School, named after one of our most prolific mines. You may know that Ferguson was one of the biggest money-making places in British Columbia at one time." He smiles, showing a hundred teeth.

"You don't say," says Grandpa.

"Well, it looks like we've come to the right place to raise a family," Bean-Trap says cheerily.

Outside, the secretaries and teachers have become very quiet.

"Now, if I could get you to fill out these forms," Mr. Phipps says, "we'll be right as rain."

Bean-Trap looks at the forms, picks up a pencil and begins, but I can see the now-familiar line of sweat glisten on his forehead. He shoves the forms over to me. "Here, you do it."

Name. What is my real name? I look at Bean-Trap, and write "Loretta Benedictson." He nods. *Former Address.* Somehow it seems ridiculous to say Weasel City, so I write "Edmonton, Alberta."

He nods again, approving my ability to muddy our trail. *Last Grade Achieved.* "Seven." *Father's Name.* "William J. Benedictson." And then the worst, *Father's Occupation.* Oh, boy. I look at Bean-Trap. Mr. Phipps leans forward to see what's stumping me. Bean-Trap takes the pencil, wets the lead in his mouth, and writes "bisnessman."

Mother's Name. I write "Christina Mary Louise Benedictson." Bean-Trap gently takes the pencil from me and adds "deceased," only he spells it "diseased." I correct it, then hand the paper back to Mr. Phipps.

"Do you have Loretta's last report card?" he asks.

"Nope."

"Then we'll have to test her to see what grade level she fits into."

"Fair enough," Bean-Trap says.

Teddy's forms are completed in the same way.

"Has this boy had any schooling at all?" Mr. Phipps asks.

"I taught him," I say, and Mr. Phipps looks surprised. "He studied reading, writing, math, spelling, geography and science."

"Well then, this young man might have to be advanced! But first we'll see how he does in a classroom situation. Mrs. Louie will now take you to your classes."

Now? We can't go in to class looking like this! Our clothes are old and not very clean, my hair hasn't been properly done. Everyone will laugh. No!

"Please, can't we start tomorrow?"

Bean-Trap looks at Teddy and me and, although he seems to take in the situation, it's Grandpa who saves the day.

"The children's grandmother and I were just getting set to buy them some supplies," he says, rising to his full height and leaning two balled-up fists on the principal's desk. "You give us a list of what they need, and the kids'll be in school bright and early tomorrow morning. Today was just to take care of preliminaries."

When we get outside the building, Teddy and I let out yells! We're happy to be going to a new school, to be getting new clothes and school things: scribblers, pencils (both black and coloured), erasers, crayons and water paints, maybe even fancy pencil-boxes like I saw in the Eaton's store in Edmonton.

"Is everyone in Ferguson such a sucker?" Bean-Trap asks.

Grandpa grins and counts out on his fingers: "Lots of money, no banks, no lawyers, no highway robbers, no policemen, no sheriff–and miles of back country to hide in if any of those show up. It's a safe haven for people like us, people who need a good rest from trouble," Grandpa concludes, patting Bean-Trap on the back as we head down the main street.

Setting up our house is a bigger job than we'd figured. We need food, bedding and dishes, all the stuff we left behind when we escaped from Weasel City. Grandma lends us some things, but they don't have very much themselves.

Everything is rationed now because of the war–meat, coffee, butter, cheese, sugar, all have to be bought only when we absolutely need them. And things are so expensive! A can of peaches, or a pound of hamburger, or a bottle of ketchup are worth more around here than gold. Bean-Trap looks like he might blow up when we go to the store on our first shopping trip.

"It shouldn't take long to figure out the system," he mutters as we toss a few things onto the counter. "It's like a card game–learn the rules, then figure how to work 'em in your favour."

♦ ♦ ♦

"We're leaving soon," Grandpa announces. "I got some mining claims and me and the missus will be moving into the skid shack out on the claim. Been finding some nice sapphires. Hardest gem in the world, next to diamonds!"

"Is that why your cat is named Sapphire?" Teddy asks.

"Sure is!" Grandpa says, grinning. "Sapphires will be the next 'gold mine' here. The mines in Montana made millionaires of nearly every Joe who showed up with a pick and shovel, late 1800s, early 1900s. Then the markets died. But I know there are sapphires around here too, big blue beauties size of hens' eggs just lying around, waiting to be gathered. Some big as ten carats."

"You don't say." Bean-Trap rubs his chin. "Sapphires. Lots of mining going on, you say?"

Grandpa's eyes flicker. "Oh, I dunno. Maybe I'm just jumpin' the gun. You'll do all right here, Bean-Trap. Just don't go jumpin' my claims, you hear?"

"I'm a business man, not a miner," he snaps. "Just keeping track of new developments, is all."

He turns to us. "Well, kids, it looks like this might be our home for a long time yet."

♦ ♦ ♦

First day of school! I wake Teddy bright and early, make our breakfasts, pack lunches, and get us washed and dressed in our new clothes.

Bean-Trap doesn't come with us. "Schools make me nervous," he says. I don't know why they should. He only went to one for three years.

As Teddy and I start down the sidewalk, I have to admit that I'm frightened. Kids converge from other streets, talking and yelling as they meet. Everyone knows each other, but nobody knows us.

I take Teddy to the first grade room. His teacher is sorting papers at her desk.

"This is Teddy Braden, er, Benedictson," I say.

She doesn't look up. "Where's his registration form?"

"In the office, I guess."

"Well, get it then."

Teddy won't let go of my hand. He begins to sob. The teacher's attention has turned back to her papers. We fight our way to the front office through a maze of hallways. Kids run and push, yelling at each other, dropping books; the noise is overwhelming. There is no teacher in sight.

I approach the front desk, where the secretary looks up and smiles as if she remember us. How could she forget Teddy and I, kind of ragged and dirty, walking in with Bean-Trap and Grandpa who acted like they might hold up the place?

"You must be here for your registration papers. Here they are," she says. "My name is Mrs. Louie, by the way. Now, Loretta, Mr. Phipps has decided to try you in the eighth grade, as you say you completed seventh grade in Alaska.

Would you like me to take your little brother to his classroom so you can find yours?"

"Yes, please."

"NO!" Teddy wails and hangs onto my hand, while his other hand clenches my skirt. I could die of embarrassment. He's dangling like a spider, and blubbering all over his new shirt. He bunches up my skirt in his hand–my new blue skirt!– and wipes his face on it.

"Teddy!" I yell, and everyone looks.

We finally calm Teddy down by promising that both the secretary and I will walk him to his classroom. The teacher, Miss Whitter, is now all smiles.

"Has he had any schooling to date?" she asks.

"Just home-schooling," Mrs. Louie replies. "His sister, Loretta here, seems to have covered all the subjects with him."

"I'm sure."

Teddy gives me one last terrified look before Mrs. Louie gently removes his left hand from my skirt, I unclench his right hand from mine, and we shove him toward his new teacher. I am no longer responsible for my brother's education.

"Now, let's find your classroom, Loretta," she says. "This is a good school, but it takes a bit of time to fit in. New kids here find it hard at first but you won't be new for long. There's always someone coming or going.

She stops in the hallway, which is now quiet as we are late for class. "First were the explorers, fur-traders, prospectors, miners, stockmen and

homesteaders. Then people came to work the
mines from all over the world: the United States
and Britain, the Scandinavian countries, Poland,
the Ukraine, Italy, Yugoslavia, Holland, China.
You'll find it quite interesting."

"So I'm not the only new kid?"

She smiles. "Today you are. Many families have
been here for a long time, but there are always
new people moving in. A mining area often
attracts a transient population."

I must look worried, because she brushes her
hand across my hair and says kindly, "Don't
worry, Loretta. You're a lovely girl, and smart too,
I can tell. You'll fit in."

We continue to walk down the hall. Before she
opens the door to my new classroom she says
quietly, "If you have any trouble, don't hesitate to
call. I'm here to see that you and your brother
enjoy Ferguson, and have good experiences at
Silver Cup School. Now, go in there and dazzle
them!"

She opens the door and the hum of activity
stops dead. All eyes turn toward me. The teacher
comes to the door.

"I'd like you to meet your new student, Loretta
Benedictson," Mrs. Louie says. "Loretta, this is
your teacher, Mr. Majec. Good luck." She wiggles
her fingers in a farewell wave, and she's gone.

I stand at attention in front of the class while Mr. Majec introduces me.

"This is Loretta Benedictson. She'll be one of your classmates."

"HELLO, LORETTA!" the class choruses.

I nearly faint. When I get the nerve to look up, I see that the kids are all smiling–they actually look happy to see me! No one sneers, or appears to be about to play a trick on me. I stammer, "Hello," and Mr. Majec takes over again.

"We have a buddy-system for new students here, Loretta. Every student gets to be a buddy. It is Joan Myers' turn, so she will be yours." A girl stands up beside her desk, and Mr. Majec takes me over to her.

"You can take this desk beside Joan, and she will be with you at recess and lunch hour. She'll show you where the washrooms are–" here the kids titter, so I guess they're normal after all, "–and the gymnasium, and every other facility we have at Silver Cup school."

I sit down, and try to concentrate on Mr. Majec's teaching as he begins an English lesson.

"Robert Service was a British poet who was born in 1874 and came to Canada in 1905. He arrived in the Yukon in 1905 and started writing poetry while he worked as a bank clerk and...."

The class groans.

"No, no, you mustn't think that because his writing is almost forty years old that it's boring," he says, holding up his hand. "He was a bank clerk in Whitehorse and Dawson City, in Canada's Yukon Territories. He was captivated by the characters who came north seeking gold."

Hey, that's my old home! I sit up and really begin to listen.

"Mr. Service went on to write poems about the Klondike Gold Rush that became quite famous. You've perhaps read 'The Shooting of Dan McGrew,' or 'The Cremation of Sam McGee,' published in 1907 in a collection titled *Songs of a Sourdough.*

"But one of my favourite poems is 'The Spell of the Yukon.' I'll read a verse or two, and I want you to think about, and compare it to, the Lardeau valley. I'm sure you'll see that Service's poems also describe people and places that you know."

He begins to read, and his voice is quiet, yet powerful:

I wanted the gold, and I sought it;
  I scrabbled and mucked like a slave.
Was it famine or scurvy–I fought it;
  I hurled my youth into a grave.
I wanted the gold, and I got it,
  Came out with a fortune last fall,–
Yet somehow life's not what I thought it
  And somehow the gold isn't all.

Mr. Majec continues and I realize I, too, have seen "a land where the mountains are nameless, and the rivers all run God knows where," and I have met the kind of people whose lives seem "erring and aimless." And I certainly know about "deaths that just hang by a hair."

I think about the snow-capped peaks of the Rocky Mountains that run from Alaska and the Yukon, down through British Columbia, and through the United States all the way to New Mexico. I only have to look out the window to see that they've followed me–or I've followed them– right to Ferguson.

Mr. Majec begins talking about line length and rhyme scheme, and I try to concentrate. After class, I ask if I can borrow the book he's been reading from.

The morning passes quickly. Mr. Majec makes every subject interesting, even math. I am quite a bit behind this class in math and science, but not in reading, or grammar, or geography.

At noon I grab my satchel and follow Joan to

the lunch room. It's so loud! The two supervisors can't begin to silence the kids, so they just make sure no one gets too rowdy. There's some food-throwing, but not too much. Joan and I take chairs side-by-side at a long table near the back. "It's for older kids," Joan says importantly.

Joan is about three inches taller than me, and a good twenty pounds heavier. I wouldn't like to tackle her in a fight, that's for sure, and from the respect she gets from other kids, they must feel the same way.

"We've lived here two years now," Joan informs me. "My Dad owns a clothing store on Windsor Street. You might have seen it. It's called Sal's Fashions for the Family."

"Yes, we went there yesterday to buy school clothes."

"Oh, good. You probably met Mom or Dad, then. They're going to take me to the movies when we go to the city next month. What's your favourite movie?" she asks.

"Where I come from there aren't any movie theatres, nothing. But I did see a magic lantern picture show once." She looks at me like I'm from the moon. "We lived in the mountains, like here only more remote, like the places described in Robert Service's poem."

"Really?"

"Yes. In fact, the people he writes about could have been our neighbours."

"Wow!" she says, suitably impressed.

I hear a commotion from the far side of the lunch room. A fight. Joan doesn't even look up from peeling her orange, but I do.

I stand up, and at first I can't see anything because everyone else is standing too. I climb onto my chair, and then I see a tousled head of hair being yanked back and forth by large boy. The little kid's nose is bleeding and he's yelling at the tops of his lungs.

I jump from my chair and push my way to the front. "Get out of my way! He's my brother!"

When I finally get to Teddy, it's all over. A supervisor is holding each boy by his arm. Both have bloody noses, and it's hard to tell who got the worst of it.

I run up to Teddy, but he turns away. His eyes are dark and flashing, and for an instant I see a reflection of Bean-Trap's fury. I take out a hand-kerchief to wipe his nose, but he pushes my hand away. "I'm okay. Leave me alone."

A bigger boy–a student lunchroom monitor– takes Teddy by the shoulder and guides him out of the room and down the hall to the boys' wash-room. I turn to a kid standing beside me. "What was that about?"

"Aw, the little guy started mouthing off. He bet Joey that he could beat him in a card game of 'Fish' after lunch. Joey says okay. Then the little guy tries to get everyone to put money on it! Money! Where's a first grader going to get money to bet on cards?"

The informer, who is about ten or eleven, looks disgusted. "Kids these days!" he snorts, and leaves me standing there by myself.

After school I pick up Teddy, whose slightly swollen nose is the only indication of his fight. Joan has asked us to walk downtown with her so she can show us her store. She goes there every day at four o'clock because her whole family works there.

The day is cloudy and cold, with a few inches of snow covering the ground. It's good to have my first day at the new school over with. I can't believe it's gone so well. Even Teddy likes it, fight and all.

"Miss Whitter isn't so bad," he says, as he trots along beside us. "The kids say she's kind of cranky, but you get used to it. You know, like–"

"Sshh!" I give a little push on his shoulder to shut him up.

We turn a corner and I suddenly grab Teddy's shoulder again. Bean-Trap is in front of us and, though he doesn't see us, we have him in full view. He's all dressed up and smoking a cigar and talking rather loudly, like he's had a bit to drink.

He has a woman on his arm. Her hair is brassy blonde and piled in curls on top of her head. Her eyebrows are arched like rainbows, setting off poppy-red lipstick and dangling rhine-stone earrings. She wears a fur piece wrapped around her shoulders, its little head biting its own tail. Her stylish short coat shows off a red silk dress, shear stockings with dark seams up the back, and high-heeled, open-toed red shoes.

"Wow!" Teddy says.

I grab his arm, and we bunch in behind Joan, heads down, walking as if we're in a hurry. We pass Bean-Trap and the woman without them seeing us, but I hear her breathe, "Oh, Bill, you're such a kidder!" He laughs in a throaty way, "You ain't seen nothin' yet!"

At home that night, I read one of Robert Service's poems. It could have been written about Bean-Trap. It's called 'The Men that Don't Fit In.'

> There's a race of men that don't fit in,
> A race that can't stay still;
> So they break the hearts of kith and kin
> And they roam the world at will.

January 30, 1943
Ferguson, BC
Dear Jay:

I hope you're enjoying school in Fairbanks as much as I am at Silver Cup school. Bean-Trap says new men are arriving in town every week to find work at the mines or stake their own claims. But many don't bring their families. They work in the day and spend their money at night—which, of course, makes Bean-Trap happy.

We now have a kitten named Angel (although he's a boy!) given to us by our "adopted" family, Grandma and Grandpa Woloshyn. I just found out yesterday that they're moving! We were invited over for supper and that's when they broke the news.

I put down my pen, and recall how happy they were to see us last night.

"How do you like school?" Grandpa asked, and Teddy and I said, "Great!" in one breath.

Grandma's face broke into a wreath of wrinkles, which meant she was smiling. *"Dobre!"* she said, which we knew meant "good" in Ukrainian.

"I got one hundred percent on my math test!" Teddy announced.

"Teh ya dobre hlopech!" Grandma said in congratulation. "Good boy."

Teddy grinned. "Yeah, I beat everyone in the class, because Dad taught me numbers a long time ago, for playing cards."

Everyone laughed.

"And how about you, Loretta?" Grandpa said. "What's your favourite subject?"

I started to tell them about Robert Service, but Bean-Trap changed the subject.

"I'm getting ready to set up a little partnership with a fellow here in town," he announced. He cupped his hand at the side of his mouth as if to prevent the news from going out of the room.

"Going to be rich in no time! You talk about sapphires lying on the ground like chicken-eggs. I'm telling you, Doc," he says to Grandpa, "this place could become the Klondike and the California gold-rush all rolled into one. Everyone's sure they'll be making money hand over fist. And they're eager to double it–on games of chance!"

He leaned forward, even more secretive. "I'm thinking of getting into dog races next. I hear that's popular down south."

Grandpa laughed, but Grandma looked over to see how I felt about these plans. I smiled, and

Grandma smiled back.

Dinner was wonderful! Grandma had made Ukrainian food: *perogies,* plump little pouches stuffed with potato, cheese and onion; and *holopchi,* which are cabbage rolls. We could eat as many as we liked because Grandma had made a dish full. She even put aside some for us to take home.

"Where did you come from before Ferguson?" I asked Grandma, as I took a third helping.

"From Edmonton," Grandpa said, with a wink.

"Is there really a country called Ukrainia?" Teddy asked.

"Both our families are from a place in Europe called Galacia," Grandma explained. "We've known each other since we were kids. Our parents first settled in the United States, but we moved to Canada just after we married."

"Do you have any kids?" Teddy asked.

"Just you two," Grandma said softly.

"We had a little boy, but he died of the flu, many years ago," Grandpa added.

"Oh. I'm sorry."

"So...now there's just the two of us. We go where we like. Nothing to tie us down." Grandma tried to laugh but her voice caught in her throat.

"We've got news, too," Grandpa said, abruptly. Grandma started carrying dishes over to the sink.

"I've finally got my claims registered," Grandpa went on. "We will be moving into the mountains next month."

"What!" Teddy and I cried in unison.

"You got a place set up already?" Bean-Trap asked, surprised.

"Good enough," Grandpa said. "It's a shack, but we'll only have one cold month, March, then it'll be spring. It will be just like camping out!"

I went over to the sink to stand beside Grandma, pretending I was helping her stack the dishes. I looked sideways, and saw tears rolling down her cheeks. They disappeared into her wrinkles, then dripped onto the collar of her new Christmas blouse, worn especially for our visit.

"Teh ya dobre dywchna," she said softly. "You are such a good girl. My good little girl." She gave me a strong hug, then turned back to the sink.

When we got ready to leave, Grandma had a surprise for us.

"It's time for you to take Angel now," she said. "Sapphire is getting tired of having a kitten running after her all day."

I picked up the lovely cream, black, and yellow kitten. He fixed me with his piercing blue eyes, and started to purr. Teddy stroked his back.

"I still don't know what we need a cat for," Bean-Trap said gruffly. "Mice are hibernating. Haven't seen a one." He caught our devastated looks, and a small smile crept across his face.

"Oh well, I guess he won't take up much room, or eat us out of house and home. Just be sure you two look after him!" He stared sternly at Teddy and me. I almost had to laugh. I've been feeding and looking after both of them for a year!

How much extra trouble could a cat be?

We said good-bye, promising to visit Grandma and Grandpa as often as we could during the next month, and help them pack their furniture and things for the move. As Grandpa drove us home Teddy and I sat between him and Bean-Trap, with Angel curled up on my lap. His loud purrs drowned out the roar of the truck's engine.

I pick up my pencil and finish the letter to Jay.

At the moment everything is going better than expected. I hope you and I can see each other again soon. Maybe, when you finish school, you and your Uncle Midnight will start your own charter airline, and fly down to the Lardeau Valley. I've written to Bugs too. Please send the letter on to him, wherever he is now. Please write soon!

Love, Loretta

◆ ◆ ◆

Sometimes Teddy and I go to Joan's parents' store with her after school or walk downtown just to look at all the other stores. Sometimes we even go for a Coca-Cola in King's cafe. Bean-Trap doesn't care. He's not fussy about what we do, or who we choose as friends, so long as they aren't connected with the law.

"That Tommy Turcott!" Joan says to me, as we stroll downtown after school. "I know he likes you. He picked you first for the spelling bee."

"That's because he knows I can spell!" I laugh.

"And at recess, he asked where you live."

"That's because he wanted me to help him carry the hamster cages he'd brought for a display."

"Really, Loretta, you're so dumb sometimes!" Joan laughs, and I punch her shoulder.

Tommy moved to town the same week we did. His father's a policeman, so he's definitely off-limits.

"I was picked to read out loud in school today," Teddy brags. "I even got to choose what to read."

"So, what did you read?" Joan asks. "*More Fun With Dick and Jane?*"

"I read a story about Noah's Ark."

Joan stops in her tracks. "What?"

"Don't you ever read the Bible?" Teddy asks. "Noah, he gets a sign that it's going to rain so he builds this big boat...."

"Yes, I know," Joan says impatiently. "I just can't believe a first grader would read that."

"I learned to read from the Bible and magazines we found in our cabin," Teddy says proudly.

"Some old trappers lived there before we did," I explain to Joan. "They left behind a Bible, so I made up Teddy's reading lessons from Bible stories."

"Yeah, so I started reading to the kids about Noah, and how people bet that he wouldn't get his boat finished in time, and then they made bets that it wouldn't float!"

"Teddy!"

"Well, Dad says that everyone gambles," Teddy continues, not noticing Joan's shocked look. "He says that even when people are in jail, they'll bet on how long it will take a fly to crawl up a wall."

"Jail?" Joan says, almost casually. "You know someone who's been in jail?"

"Not really," I say, but before I can give Teddy a warning, he pipes up, "Sure, Dad has! They call him Bean-Trap because he trapped other men's beans in his casino. And the guy who set fire to his place in Eagle went to jail! Lots of people we know have been in jail. If we hadn't come down here real quick, Dad might be in jail right now! They think he killed a man, but I bet he didn't really. And if he did, the man asked for it."

"I see." Joan stops. "Look, I just remembered, I have to run an errand for my mother. It will take me quite a while. See you," and she was off.

I know, without having to be told, that Joan Myers will never be my friend again. And after she's told other kids what Teddy said, no one else will like us either.

"Oh, Teddy!" I cry, but the lump in my throat stops me from saying any more.

"Dad told me he's going to set up a real nice place here," Teddy rattles on. "He's going to have a roulette wheel, and then bring in dogs...."

"Shut up!" I stop walking. I'm on the verge of tears. "Just shut up for once! You and your big mouth–you've just ruined my whole life!"

I stomp down the street, not caring that I can hear his feet pounding along behind me, trying to keep up.

At school the next day, things are just as bad as I figured.

"Hey! Loretta! We used to have Copper Kings here! Now I hear we got a Craps King!"

"That your old man I seen rolling dice behind Batho's store? Must have been; he had snake-eyes!"

I can't stand it. When Joan sees me coming toward her, she loses herself in a group of girls who all stare and whisper. Even Mr. Majec knows something is wrong, but he can't do anything about it. Teachers never can. I hold my head up and ignore them, even though tears burn at the back of my eyes. I wonder how Teddy is handling this, then I think, "Serves him right, whatever he gets. He'll learn not to have such a big mouth!"

I try to concentrate on Mr. Majec's lesson.

"The next class assignment, which will count for twenty-five percent of our Easter exam mark, is an essay on some aspect of our local history," Mr. Majec says. "You can write about British

Columbia's flora and fauna, its people, its history, anything you choose. Hand it in by next Monday."

◆ ◆ ◆

I somehow make it through the day. After school, I pick up Teddy in front of his classroom and make him come to the school library with me. I have to get books for my essay, and I want to avoid being taunted as we walk home.

Teddy is quiet, which is the way I prefer it.

"I know you're still mad at me, Loretta," he says, as he follows me around the library.

"I'm not mad, I'm hurt," I say, which should make him feel even more miserable. "You ought to know after Eagle, Fairbanks, and Weasel City that we can *never* talk about Bean-Trap's business. I can't believe you mouthed off in front of Joan."

"I'm sorry. I just forgot."

I kneel down so I'm at eye level with him. "Never forget again, okay? He may be different from most Dads, but he loves us, and he's all we've got."

Tears come to Teddy's eyes. I leave him sitting on a chair, while I go to the history section.

I find books on every subject from the fur trade to native migrations and settlements along both sides of the Canada-U.S. border, and then I find a subject that jumps out at me–the trek made by Chief Joseph and the Nez Perce. I check out a couple of books, and we leave to go home.

Angel is at the door to meet us. We call him

our "watch-cat," because he's just as sharp and protective of our home as a dog could be. I scoop him up in my arms.

"That cat's got a purr like a well-oiled roulette wheel!" Bean-Trap exclaims. He has supper for us: bacon, eggs and apple pancakes–his specialty!

"What's the occasion?" I ask. He grins and turns back to the grille. "Had a good night last night. Payday at the mines!"

Okay, I'm going to tell him. He should know how hard it is for us to hide from other kids what he does for a living. I'm tired of running, lying, pretending, doing all the things that I, and Teddy, have to do to protect our secret. I'm tired of being the gambler's daughter.

"Something happened yesterday...."

"It's my fault!" Teddy pipes up. "Let me tell, Loretta. Dad, I squealed."

Bean-Trap becomes pale under his unshaven whiskers. He sets down the pancake flipper and slowly turns from the grille. "You did what?"

Teddy swallows hard. Two bright red spots appear on his cheeks. "I blabbed. I talked about, you know, your business, in front of Loretta's friend, Joan Myers. Joan told everyone. Now no one will talk to us."

"Joan Myers," Bean-Trap repeats.

"Yes. My friend–my ex-best friend!" I say.

"That wouldn't be Sal Myers' kid, would it?"

"I guess so. They own Sal's Fashions for the Family downtown on Windsor Street."

He throws back his head and lets out a big guffaw. His gold teeth gleam. What's going on?

"Dad!"

He wipes the flipper on the leg of his pants and slips it beneath a big pancake, turning it expertly. He turns to face us. "Look, I ain't a squealer. Those kind end up in the river wearing concrete boots. But let me tell you a little joke. You're nobody in this town unless you've got at least one ancestor who was crooked. Understand that."

He sets the flipper on the side of the grille, pulls out a kitchen chair and sits down, facing us.

"Once upon a time there was a man who wanted to turn a dime into a dollar. He'd tried 'legit' ways–running a grocery store, a butcher shop, a clothing store–but these were penny-ante trades. He'd make a few bucks, then spend them to buy his next season's stock or fix up the shop. So he gets the idea he should 'invest' his Christmas sale money in poker. When he won, he'd have cash to expand his store, maybe take the family on a little holiday–most apples' dreams."

"Yours too?" Teddy says with a smirk.

"Well, we're worlds apart, this man and me. You see, I don't trust Lady Luck as much as he did. I hedge my bets a little–"

"Like with cold-decks!" Teddy says.

Bean-Trap looks at him curiously. "Good memory, son. Combine that with 'going on the Erie' and you'll make a good businessman. Now–"

"Going on the Erie?"

"Keeping silent. Code as old as time. Eyes and ears open, mouth shut. Now, this man, he don't know what he's up against. He plays, badly. Can't remember nothin'. Gets panicky. Bids crazy. I say to him, 'Mister, you better cool it for a night. Take your losses, go home, think about it, maybe come back in a month or so.' But no, he insists on staying, and it's no go. Dice are cold. Well, I ain't a priest, or a financial counselor, so I let him go on."

Bean-Trap stands to scoop the bacon to one side of the pan so the grease will drain, then he cracks a half-dozen eggs. They sizzle as they hit the hot pan.

"So what happened to this man?" I ask.

"Well, you might see a certain store go up for sale here pretty quick. It's a sad story, but one based on stupidity and greed. So don't get thinking you're not as good as some other people. Everyone's got skeletons in their closets, everyone's got secrets. You ain't no rabbit–so don't run like one."

"You mean, it was Joan's father? Are the Myers' going to lose the store?"

He holds up his hand. "No! No! 'Go on the Erie,' remember? Ears and eyes open–mouth shut. But if you get hassled by anyone, you tell me, okay?"

I nod. Angel has stopped purring, as if he, too, has been listening to the story–or maybe it's just the bacon grease that has captured his attention.

We eat a supper fit for a king. The wood blazes in the cook-stove, the food is delicious, and there are no cards in sight.

◆   ◆   ◆

On Monday, I hand in my essay. The following day, Mr. Majec motions for me to stay after class.

"That's quite a piece you wrote, Loretta," he says. "It deserves the 'A' that I've given it. It brings out a very important, though perhaps shameful, aspect of North American history. I'd like you to read it to the class. Do you think you could do that?"

Oh, boy. Many of the kids' families have lived on both sides of the border–perhaps they were part of the problems! But, no one is speaking to me now, so what does it matter if they like me even less after my essay is read?

CHIEF JOSEPH AND THE NEZ PERCE
by Loretta Benedictson

In 1877, the U.S. federal government tried to force the Nez Perce (which means "pierced nose") Indians out of their home in north-eastern Oregon, so that white settlers could have their fertile and valuable lands. That started the Nez Perce Wars.

Eight hundred Indians, their leaders including Chief Joseph, and horses headed through Washington, Idaho, and Montana, then north through what's now called Yellowstone Park. They were trying to reach Canada, where they felt they would be treated better.

But the army followed, and battles were fought along the trail. The Nez Perce fought bravely because they were armed with pride, hope–and humour. When they camped, even though they were hungry and death stared them in the face, they told jokes so that their tired minds and bodies could relax.

The army caught up to them forty-five miles from the Canadian border at Bear's Paw Canyon. The Battle of Bear's Paw lasted four horrible days, in cold, snowy weather.

After Chief Looking Glass and Joseph's brother had been shot, and others, including children, were dead, wounded, freezing or starving, Chief Joseph had to call it quits.

"Hear me, my chiefs, I am tired," he said. "My heart is sick and sad. From where the sun now stands, I will fight no more."

Chief Joseph, whose Indian name means "Thunder Travelling Across a Lake and Fading on the Mountainside," died in 1904. Some say he died of a broken heart.

The years since this battle have been very hard for native people of North America.

Before Mr. Majec or the kids can say anything, I decide to head right into it. "I have another story about injustice, but it's not written here," I say.

The room is silent. All eyes are on me.

"A gambler made a bet with the Devil that he'd find on his travels an honest man; the Devil bet he couldn't. He at last came to British Columbia, where he decided to test people, one by one beginning with the important people.

"The Devil found that the gambler himself was one of the most honest people around–because he admitted what he did for a living, while others lied and tried to hide it."

I look over the class, at Tommy Turcotte who has a slight smile on his face, at Joan Myers whose eyes are downcast, at the rest of the kids who look at each other and then at Mr. Majec. Then someone starts to titter. I see a smile begin to break over Joan's face. Tommy Turcotte lets out a big guffaw. The sound builds, from one side of the room to the other, until the class, and Mr. Majec too, join in the laughter.

Joan stands up and begins to clap. Others, not quite sure of what's going on stand too, and applaud as I walk back to my desk beside Joan's.

I think back to the friends I've had, and it seems strange that Joan is the first one my age. I played with kids in the early grades, but after Eagle our home life became so different that I couldn't bring friends home, and Bean-Trap didn't like me going to other people's houses.

Millie and I were as different as two people could be–we didn't even share a language, but that didn't seem to matter. I still feel very close to her, even though I can't write to her because she couldn't read my letter, and because Bean-Trap insists that we don't contact people from the past. I know he's 'on the lam' here. He still hasn't said why we had to leave Weasel City and neither Teddy nor I have the nerve to ask.

I really miss Grandma and Grandpa Woloshyn too. She liked the Liberty Hotel, the miners and thought she'd found a permanent home. Why do women always have to follow men around? I won't leave my home and friends when a man gets a crazy idea and tells me to pack up.

I told Jay and Bugs to send my letters in care of the Liberty Hotel because I didn't know how long we'd be here and I knew Grandma would send them on. But, strangely enough, Grandma was the first to leave. Now, what if they've written to me and I don't get the letters? After school, I'll ask the new owners if anything has come for me.

This morning, Joan sent me a note, "Important stuff to talk about at recess."

Joan and I go over to the far fence where we won't be overheard. "I'm going to tell you a secret. You can't tell anybody else," she says.

"I promise."

"We're moving! Dad is selling the store and we're going to Trail. His brother has a store there, and Dad's becoming a partner. Isn't that exciting?"

My heart is racing, and I can hardly speak. "Yeah. I'll miss you though. When are you going?"

"Easter break. Oh, Loretta, I'll miss you too! But we can write, okay? Like pen-pals? Like you and Jay and Bugs?"

"Sure."

After school, Teddy and I walk downtown with Joan. "Come in for a minute," she says. I'm about to say no, when Mrs. Myers comes outside. "Oh, hello, Loretta. Hello, Teddy."

"Mom's thrilled to be moving to Trail," Joan says to me in a low voice. "Her family lives there, and it's a really busy place, not like here. You'll have to come and visit us sometime."

Teddy and I continue down the street. "What did Joan say to you?" Teddy asks. "I hate it when people whisper and I can't hear."

"You don't deserve to be let in on secrets, big-mouth," I answer.

The people who now run the Liberty Hotel are younger than Grandma and Grandpa, and very business-like. "Yes, a letter did come for someone named Loretta, but the last name was Braden, not Benedictson," the man says. "I was going to return it to the sender, because I didn't know anyone by the name of Braden."

I admit that it's for me, even though I know Bean-Trap would have a fit.

"That was my father's name, before he died," I say quickly. "There may be more letters. I'll come again to check."

"Right-o!"

"Have you heard from Mr. and Mrs. Woloshyn since they moved?" I ask.

"Nah. We won't be hearin' from them for a while. Their shack's somewhere out in the bush, nothing around but mountains, trees, and—he should hope—some precious gems to scrape out of the ground. Their only company is the bears or deer!" He laughs. "We're getting lots of bills in for them, though. Mr. Woloshyn liked to spend more than he brought in. No wonder they're hiding out!"

I grab Teddy and we stomp down the stairs. I don't care if I wake up every one of his roomers. I won't come here again. I'll tell Jay and Bugs to send their letters to General Delivery, Ferguson, B.C. We'll be here for a long time yet.

Bean-Trap isn't home when Teddy and I arrive. Angel runs to meet us, and I pick him up and hand him over to Teddy. I go to the outhouse, lock the door and sit down with my letter.

March 5, 1943
Fairbanks, Alaska
Dear Loretta:

I was glad to get your letter. You sound very happy. I was worried. Ferguson, B.C., is a long way from Fairbanks if I had to come to rescue you!

You're having a better time at school than I am. I was quite a bit behind from working at the mill. It's hard to study English (yuck) and Geography (not so bad) and Math (which I like) and Science (real hard) by correspondence!

I have some sad news. Bugs was hurt badly at our mill at the Liard River. His foot had to be amputated. He is back in Edmonton now.

Uncle Midnight crashed his plane, but he's okay now and has bought another one. The Alaska Highway got finished on schedule, and you should see all the traffic (the moose are scared!).

Say hi to Teddy and Angel for me. I don't know when I'll see you again, but maybe I will go into business with my uncle Midnight....

I miss you. Keep writing. Your letters cheer me up.
Love, Jay

"Loretta, who's making supper?" Teddy bangs on the door. I tuck the letter away, unlock the door and come back to the house. I manage to sneak Jay's letter into my treasure-box, where it will be safe from prying eyes before I begin making supper.

It gets dark around seven o'clock so I fill the lamp with fuel, trim the wick and when it's lit, I guard the flame so it doesn't leap up the chimney and leave charcoal trails.

Teddy and I have just settled down to do homework and play with his train when Angel suddenly arches his back and stiffens his legs.

"What's the matter, Angel?"

He stalks toward the door, growling.

"Angel, smarten up!"

"He's trying to tell us something. Did you lock the door?"

"I can't remember."

I stand up to check, and at that moment someone pounds on the door. My heart leaps, and begins racing like crazy. "Sshh!"

The cat is stalking back and forth, his tail switching. His low angry snarls send electrical currents through the air. The pounding increases until the door shakes on its hinges.

I stand against it, and say, "Who's there?" in the bravest voice I can manage.

"Friend of your dad's! Need to see him. He in?"

Bean-Trap has told us to never admit that we're alone. But how can I say he's here when he's not? "Maybe..." I answer.

"Let me in! He told me to come here to see him."

"I can't!"

Thump! Crash! Wood splinters! The door springs open, knocking me across the room. I scream as a sharp pain burns my shoulder like a hot wire. Teddy jumps up and his train crashes off the track. A man stands in the open doorway. Cold wintry air whips around him.

"I'm looking for Bean-Trap Braden!"

It's been a long time since I've heard that name.

"He's not here!" Teddy says.

"Zat so? Well, now. Maybe I can collect anyway."

I get to my feet, holding my arm. I think my shoulder is cracked, or pulled out of the socket. I feel sick.

"What do you want?"

"Your old man owes me, big. I lost a bundle to him in Alaska, in Weasel City, and here again. Braden, Benedictson, whatever he's called, a snake's a snake! He come home braggin' about his big win?"

"No."

"I been slavin' in that mine. Your old man beat me out of every red cent. And I'm here to collect."

"It's nothing to do with us! We didn't cheat you! He works downtown."

"Oh, I know where he works, all right! He's not here?" He looks around, wildly. He's either drunk or crazy, or both. My heartbeat has slowed a little. I see Angel slither under the table. If only he could talk, get help!

"I done some checkin' on Bean-Trap Braden! He pays me back, or I turn him in. He's runnin' from the law! He murdered Black Mike Michaluk back in Weasel City!"

"No!"

"My contacts got their ears to the ground! Bean-Trap is wanted in Alaska, he's wanted in northern B.C., and he's wanted here–by me! I'll kill the sonofa...." He stops, mid-word, and a cunning look comes over his face. "Maybe killin's too good for him...."

He reaches out and his fingers snag the little silver locket Bean-Trap gave me for Christmas. The chain snaps and it flies across the room.

"Get out!"

"Not till I even the score with your old man. You're just the daughter of a two-bit cheatin' gambler! You're not worth nothin'!" He catches me by my sore shoulder, and I jump, but not fast enough. He slams me up against the wall. Teddy claws at him. I can feel the man's heart beat, I can smell drink and tobacco and sweat and anger.

I'm crying, but I hear Teddy scream, the cat yowl, and then–a rush of air, a bullish roar, and Bean-Trap comes flying across the room. He lands on the man's back, nearly crushing my rib cage. The plaster and laths on the wall give way and I fall into a hollow between two wall-joists.

I slump to the floor as the two men roll around, fists pounding, legs intertwining, tripping, falling, grunting, their curses fouling the air. Teddy is bawling and Angel has gone wild, racing from one side of the room to the other. I look around for a weapon to protect myself and Teddy. I grab the coat rack that stands by the door so the coats fall to the floor in a heap. I hold the rack in front of me like a knight's lance, ready to charge.

The man gains his feet, lunges toward the stove, and grabs the long-handled iron poker. He swings, it whistles through the air, and whack! It connects with the side of Bean-Trap's head. His knees buckle, then he lets out a holler and attacks, knees bent, head first, crashing into the man's gut. The man grunts as the wind is knocked out of him. The poker whips into the air, somersaults, and clatters onto the hot stove. The man's head hits the corner of the stove. As he slumps to the floor a gun falls out of his boot, and he lies there motionless.

Bean-Trap rocks back and forth on his hands and knees and then collapses on the floor. Teddy and I are silent.

I set down the coat rack, and close the door as best I can against the night cold. I hear the foot-steps of neighbours and someone yells, "Tell Constable Turcotte they're over here!" I grab a dishtowel and hold it against Bean-Trap's head. He wavers in and out of consciousness. He comes to for a moment and whispers hoarsely, "Get out of here–take Teddy–I'll find you."

The man hasn't moved. I crawl toward him cautiously. His mouth is open, but his breath is low and unsteady. The side of his head is bruised and bulging where he hit the edge of our stove.

Teddy begins to whimper. The cat creeps over to Bean-Trap, touches a foot lightly to his leg and peers up at him with steady blue eyes. The clock ticks, the stove wood crackles, Teddy makes little animal-like noises, Bean-Trap breathes heavily through his mouth, and I sit very still.

I rinse a towel in cold water and wipe his face. The other man still hasn't moved. One of Teddy's train cars is smashed, stomped on during the fight. The hole in the wall, and the broken laths and plaster, give testimony to the struggle. I see strands of my blonde hair in the broken plaster.

I start to wipe the blood off the stove, then stop. Maybe it can be used as evidence.

"Let's go, Teddy!"

He turns a tear-stained face to me, then looks back at his Dad. "Where can we go, Loretta? We can't leave him."

"We can't help him now. I'm not a doctor or a lawyer. He said we should go. Come on!"

I grab my treasure box, Angel, our duffel bags, coats and some money from our hiding spot and we make a run for it. I'll think of what to do once we're out of this house.

"Dad's always found us before. He can look after himself."

I shove a duffel bag into Teddy's hand and push him down the side path. We have no choice but to run!

We creep down to the railway roundhouse where the trains shuttle around, some going north and some going south, loaded or empty from hauling ore. Do we buy a ticket? Do we try to jump into an empty car going anywhere, and ride like hobos?

Teddy is whining. "Loretta, I don't want to go! I like it here! I don't wanna leave Dad!"

"Be quiet! We can't stay. You saw that man, and you heard Bean-Trap tell us to get out. He'll find us, don't worry."

"He'll find us where? We don't even know where we're going. How can we leave a message?"

He's right. I stop to think. All around us the dark buildings of main street offer protection. I can hear people laughing somewhere, and dogs barking. The hills beyond the town are quiet. I don't want to leave Ferguson either.

"Maybe we can find Grandma and Grandpa," Teddy says.

"I wish I knew where they were. But, we can leave a message for Grandma and Grandpa at the Liberty. When they come to town for groceries, they'll stay there and they'll get in touch with Bean-Trap. Then he'll have an idea where to come and look for us."

Teddy sniffles and wipes his tears on his coat sleeve. I put down my baggage and hold Teddy in my arms. I can feel his heart beating rapidly, even through his coat. He's so small, and we're so alone.

I say in a firm voice, "Teddy, where would you like to go? Let's pretend this is an adventure."

"I want to go back to Edmonton," Teddy says. "I want to go to Eaton's and see their trains. I want to see Bugs! He's there!"

"Wow! That's a great idea." Bean-Trap has opened a bank account for us there! It all makes perfect sense. "Let's go to Edmonton, then!" I say brightly. "But first we'll write that message."

"Yeah?" Teddy says, his tears quickly drying. "A secret message, written in a code like in the comic books? The bad guys leave coded messages under rocks, or carved on trees, so only their friends can read them...."

"Yes, yes, just like that," I reply. "Now, as Bean-Trap would say, 'Go on the Erie'. We have work to do."

The train station is at the end of the street. We can hopefully get a ticket and be on our way tonight. The only route I can think to take to Edmonton is the way we came. We have enough money, that's no problem. I approach the ticket master with bravado, but he doesn't even blink at two kids buying a one-way ticket to Spokane. "Train's leaving in an hour," he says, and turns back to his newspaper.

"Excuse me," I say. He looks up from his paper. "Do you have a piece of paper and a pen? I want to leave a message for friends at the hotel. I'll give you a dollar to have it delivered."

He rummages around and finds us some paper with "Canadian Pacific Railway" printed on the top.

"Dear Grandma and Grandpa," I write. *"Do you remember the sign that Dad said you'd some-day put up on the hotel? Well, he truly is famous. When you see him, please tell him we've gone to buy more train cars and a new locket. We hope you are well. Love, your grandchildren."*

I get the ticket master's attention again and hand him the folded letter. He shoves it into an envelope, which I address to Mr. and Mrs. Woloshyn in care of the Liberty Hotel, with PLEASE HOLD FOR PICK-UP underlined twice.

We wait outside in the crisp cool autumn night, watching peoples' house lights blink off, one after another. Soon, a full moon rises over the eastern hills to bathe Ferguson in a wash of silver.

I have our birth certificates ready as we cross the border. "Go on the Erie!" I warn Teddy. In the busy train car, with single miners and families and kids filling the seats and aisles, we are assumed to be part of someone's family and aren't even questioned. Whew!

In Spokane we buy a cage for Angel, to keep her from jumping out *en route*. We also purchase enough food to get us by. Teddy is quiet. He plays with his little broken train car, occasionally responding to my chirpy comments about how nice it will be to replace his broken car with a shiny new one.

"Don't worry," I say. "As soon as we get to Edmonton we'll find a nice place to live, just the two of us, and wait." But I can't help wondering how we're ever going to rent a place. No one would rent to kids. If people find we're on our own, they'll call the welfare office and we'll end up in an orphanage. I'm really frightened, but I can't let on to Teddy.

"I want to see Bugs," Teddy says suddenly. "I liked him. He lives in Edmonton. Maybe he'll help us."

"Maybe he will," I murmur, more to soothe Teddy than anything else.

We buy tickets to take the train from Spokane to Great Falls. It takes a long time, with many stops in towns and cities along the way, but we don't get off. I'm afraid we might get lost. Maybe the police are looking for us.

Teddy falls asleep with his head against my arm. When he shouts "Daddy! Daddy, come home!" during a nightmare I say quietly, "Shhh, shhh, everything will be okay."

I too am thinking of "Daddy" and my refusal to call him that, even when Mom asked me to, until the name "Bean-Trap" became a "trap" for all of us. I finger the broken silver locket that is safely tucked in my pocket, and think of the gold earrings that had once been Mom's. I think of Weasel City, and of Millie and Pete and the kids.

I think of Ferguson, and Grandma and Grandpa Woloshyn, and wonder if they've found any gems. I imagine their reaction when they get my note at the Liberty Hotel. Then I think of Ferguson, and how I loved my school. Maybe someday I'll be able to write to Mr. Majec, or to Joan. Perhaps someday we'll be back.

I also think of Jay, and Bugs. I'm glad I was able to grab my treasure box, containing their letters. Teddy is right. Bugs might be able to help us; we sure need it.

The train rolls through the states of Washington and Idaho into Montana. As we approach Great Falls, I begin to worry about the next part of the trip, crossing the U.S. border back into Canada. For some reason, kids riding alone on the train in this part of the country seems to attract more attention than on the Ferguson to Spokane leg of the journey. Passengers stare at us, and some even ask us where are parents are.

"We're going to visit our aunt," I lie, and look busy arranging our bags.

We disembark in Great Falls and walk across

the street to a hotel and coffee shop. We're tired of bread, cheese and baloney, chocolate bars and pop, our food for the past two days. We take a back booth in the coffee shop and try to ignore the curious stares.

As we wait for our order of tomato soup, grilled ham sandwiches and chocolate milk-shakes, I notice the waitress looking over at us. She is talking to a man sitting on a stool at the counter. He nods, looks over at us, and comes to our booth.

"Hey, kids, Molly and I couldn't help noticing that you seem to be kind of lost," the man says. "I'm Bill Docherty, by the way. I drive a truck. Molly, here, the waitress, is an old friend of mine. Do you mind us asking where you're heading?"

"We're going to our aunt's place, in Edmonton," I blurt out.

"Edmonton? Across the border? You taking the bus?"

"I don't know," I say, less confidently.

"You're not running away, are you?" He nods to the waitress and she brings over his coffee. "Now, why don't you tell me what brings you two to Great Falls?"

Giving Teddy a warning again to "Go on the Erie," I make up a story. It's partly based on truth, but keeps Bean-Trap's name completely out of it. I tell Bill that our mom is in the hospital in Butte, our dad is overseas fighting in the war, and our aunt in Edmonton has offered to take care of us. She can't come for us because her husband, our uncle, is sick, so we've got to get there on our own. I can feel my face flush, and I'm sure Bill can tell I'm making this up as I go along.

"So, our aunt is expecting us," I finish lamely. "I guess we can take the bus across the border. We have the money."

He gives me a look that says, 'Okay, kid, don't take it too far,' and takes a sip of his coffee.

"You'll have to have your birth certificates on you, and a guardian who can take you across," he says finally. "They don't let kids run from one country to another on their own you know."

My breathing becomes shaky. What are we going to do?

"I don't know your real story, but I trust you have reasons for being where you are," he says, "and I'm willing to help you. Some friends of mine, Joe Hofer in particular, cross the border nearly every week. These people are seldom stopped. I think they might be convinced to help you."

We pay for our food–even though Bill offers to–gather up our stuff, including Angel who's been scratching around inside the cage, and go out to Bill's rig parked in the back parking lot.

"Wow!" says Teddy, as we clamber up some high steps into the cab. Bill drives us to a part of town where we see large corrals of cattle and barns.

"This is the stockyard," he says. "I see Mr. Hofer's rig over by the weigh scale. You kids wait here while I go and have a chat with him. I'll find out when he plans to leave, then try to convince him to give you a ride."

In ten minutes he returns with three men dressed in bright-coloured cotton shirts, black jackets and pants, black boots, and black hats. Two of the men have beards, but the youngest one, who looks about sixteen, doesn't. "These are the kids, Loretta and Teddy," Bill Docherty says. "Can you get them to Lethbridge?"

The men talk among themselves in a language we've never heard before. Finally they say one word we do understand, and have been hoping to hear, "Yes."

"These people are Hutterites," Bill explains. "They live on big community farms, called colonies. Joe Hofer is the boss of a big spread just outside of Lethbridge."

"What language are they speaking?" I ask. "I can't understand them."

"German," Bill replies, "but most of them also speak English. You won't have any problems understanding. I don't speak German, but I was able to convince them that you kids need help. They're good people. They'll take care of you."

I guess Teddy and I look pretty worried because Bill kneels down beside Teddy and says, "Everything's going to be just fine, little fella. You and your sister might have an uncomfortable ride ahead of you, but it won't last forever. You'll be in Lethbridge in a few hours, and you can take the train from there through Calgary to Edmonton. You have enough money?"

"Yes." Teddy snuffles. I hadn't realized he was so close to tears.

The Hutterite men stare at us. One man comes forward and lifts a tarp on the back of the truck, indicating that we are to clamber inside.

He throws in our bags, then drops in Angel in his cage. But the moment he does that, shrieks and the most awful squawking sounds rise up inside the truck-box. We jump, scared out of our wits! In the dark, we hear Angel spitting and snarling inside her cage; this sets off an answering round. Honk! Gaggle, gaggle, gaggle! Honk!

Mr. Hofer and the other two men laugh.

"Geese!" He lifts the flap and we suddenly meet our riding companions.

"Oh, no!"

Stacks of wooden crates hold big grey geese. The noise is wild, and straw and feathers fly everywhere. Mr. Hofer leans inside, indicates a little nest in the straw up near the cab and motions for us to crawl in. "You sit here, good. We stop at Sweetgrass, before border, see how you do."

We catch on. We are to hide in the straw, behind the goose crates. One thing we won't have to worry about is being quiet. No one could hear us over forty live geese, especially with a cat thrown in.

"Honk! Honk! yourselves!" Teddy yells.

I have to laugh.

It's warm in here because of their body heat and the straw. And it's a comfy place to sleep. The geese settle down when we get moving, and even Angel seems to relax, although cats seldom do. I remove the cloth covering his cage. It's dark inside the tarp-covered truck so I can't see him, but I know he's watching every move the geese make. They are birds, after all.

"Loretta?" I can barely hear Teddy's voice.

"Yes?"

"I'm scared."

I draw him close. "We'll be okay, and so will Bean-Trap. The police aren't going to hurt him. He'll maybe spend some time in a jail, then he'll come for us. Don't worry."

"Okay." He knows this is our only choice.

Soon Teddy is asleep. I snuggle down beside him, my layers of clothing and the straw keeping me warm. I am almost asleep when I start to think, and to worry.

I imagine that the spinning truck wheels are singing a song, "Guilt! Guilt! Guilt! Bad! Bad! Bad!" This is crazy. What do I have to feel guilty, or bad, about? None of this is my fault! But my brain won't quit.

I recall a lesson we were taught in Social Studies. "In Canada, every person controls his own destiny," Mr. Majec said. We were to discuss that statement.

Everyone talked about the freedom we have in

this country to make our fortunes, no matter what kind of family we come from or how much money we have when we start out.

Where has destiny got Bean-Trap–or us? Ever since Mom married him we've been on the run from one place to another, and not very nice places, either–shacks and cabins and old houses that no one else wanted.

And we've been on the run from the law, too, from Eagle, and Fairbanks, and Weasel City, and now from Ferguson.

I really believe I love Bean-Trap, but I don't think he's been that smart, or that lucky. So far, he hasn't pulled the nine of diamonds.

I think of the job ahead of me, looking after Teddy and myself for the next few years, or until Bean-Trap gets out of jail. I'll be seventeen or eighteen. Will I still be in school? Or will I have to quit to go to work?

Teddy will be nine or ten when Bean-Trap gets out. He will likely still think of him as a hero because he's had no other man to learn from, to teach him any differently.

I could go crazy thinking like this! I decide to think about good things: like Jay. Right now he's in school in Fairbanks, Alaska, trying to get good marks so he can become a pilot. Perhaps some day he, or Midnight Smith, can fly us all over the place.

Bugs is a good person, too. I only met him once, but his eyes crinkled when he laughed, and he did that lots. It was fun getting his letters. I wonder how he's managing with his injured foot. I hope we can find him.

My brain slows as sleep drifts in. I hear Angel stir in his cage.

♦　♦　♦

I am awakened when the truck stops, its doors slamming, and the men get out. Mr. Hofer lifts the flap. "How are you?" he calls.

"Fine." I crawl toward the open flap. The light makes my eyes water. I blink like a mole.

"You have straw in your hair! You look like a calf!" he laughs. "Come outside, you and brother, walk around. Get something to eat. We are in Sweetgrass."

The men share their sandwiches with us. They're delicious! The other two men are shy around us and don't speak much. I decide to let Angel out to stretch, but I tie my hair ribbons around his neck and use a long one for a leash in case he takes off. There's no way I'd leave him behind!

We get back into the truck, and cover ourselves with straw and an old tarp as Mr. Hofer instructs us to. This is the scariest part of the ride. Teddy and I can hardly talk over the sound of the truck engine, and it's just as well. I haven't much to say to reassure him. If we're caught, the Hofers can hardly say we're their kids! They will have to say they didn't know we were back there.

The truck slows, then stops, although the loud engine keeps running. I hear an inspector talk to Mr. Hofer, although I can't make out what they are saying. Then the truck door opens and I hear Mr. Hofer come around the back. He lifts the flap. I burrow deep into the straw, clutching Teddy's hand. We barely breathe.

"Geese!" Mr. Hofer says. "Forty-two geese! Want one for next Christmas?" He laughs.

"And that's all?" the border inspector says.

"That all. Oh yeah..." My breathing stops. "...and one cat. For the mice!"

"You have papers for transporting these birds?"

"Yes."

The tarp falls down again, and I hear Mr. Hofer rope it into place, then return to the cab to get his papers. In minutes the truck door slams shut, Mr. Hofer shifts the engine into first gear, and the old truck lurches ahead.

It's over. We're in Canada.

I pull two cookies from my coat pocket. Mr. Hofer had given them to us at lunch.

"Here, Teddy, let's celebrate!"

We gnaw on the cookies, breaking off little chunks for Angel, which he eats hungrily. I offer a piece to one of the geese, too. Then the others start clamouring for a piece and they become so loud that we laugh and shout, trying to be even louder. It's a wonder Mr. Hofer doesn't stop the truck, thinking we've gone mad back here. But we're not mad–we're joyously happy. We're free!

◆　◆　◆

The truck rumbles on and I fall asleep again. When I awake I can hear no engine sounds. We've stopped. I sit up, pulling straw out of my hair, then peek out a small hole in the tarp to see where we are. Around us are big buildings like barns. We're in some kind of a stock yard. I want to crawl out but don't dare.

Finally I hear voices. "Take them to weigh scale," Mr. Hofer says.

There is silence again, then the flap is lifted. "You can come out now," Mr. Hofer says to us. "Lethbridge."

Teddy and I push our bags and Angel's cage to the tailgate and Mr. Hofer takes them. We climb out and jump to the ground. My legs nearly buckle. I brush straw off myself and Teddy, and he brushes my back where I can't reach. It's amazing how presentable we look after our long ride.

"The train is there," Mr. Hofer says, pointing. The tracks run along the stock yards where he has parked. We thank him and follow the tracks for a few blocks to the station. The station master tells us that a train going north to Calgary will be here in about an hour; from there we can go on to Edmonton.

Only when we're sitting in the Pullman car,

with our bags around us and Angel in his cage on the floor, do I begin to relax a bit. The train is jam-packed with soldiers. One gives Teddy some "Sad Sack" and "Joe Palooka" comic books.

I don't hear a word from him until a man comes down the aisle selling sandwiches and soft drinks, and Teddy and I realize we're starving. We wolf down the sandwiches, followed by two candy bars each given to us by the soldiers.

We disembark in Calgary, and watch as the military men wave good-bye. They are going on to Vancouver. We have three hours to wait until the next train to Edmonton. We check our bags, and go for a walk. We go into a little grocery store, buy some apples, and pay for them with an American bill. The man grumbles a bit but gives us our change in Canadian money. It will be enough to get us to Edmonton, where our real Canadian money is stored in the vaults of the bank on Jasper Avenue.

◆　◆　◆

Edmonton is so busy! Airplanes circle in the air, landing and taking off from the big airport at the north end of the city.

"Some of those airplanes are going north to Alaska, and then over to Russia," a man informs Teddy when he sees us looking skyward. Alaska! We watch a flock of Canada geese fly over, in a big "V" formation.

"I wonder if we could catch a ride on one of those geese?" I say to Teddy. "We should be able to speak their language!"

"Are they going north, Loretta? To Weasel City? To Alaska? Home?"

♦ ♦ ♦

The first thing we do in Edmonton is get a room, in the same hotel we stayed in with Bean-Trap at Christmas. And it's the same hotel desk clerk! "I remember you," he says, smiling. "You're the Benedictson children!"

"That's right. Our Dad will be coming later. Can we get a room now, please? We can pay for it." I give him American money, and he takes it without a problem.

"Your cat," he says, pointing to Angel who is pressing his face against the bars of the cage. "He'll have to be kept in the basement, I'm afraid. But he'll be warm and dry, and fed and watered by the staff–and a litter box is provided."

"Thank you!" I say, as Teddy is about to protest. I honestly can't think how we'd have managed to find a litter box in a hotel room, and the results could be disastrous.

When we are up in our room with the door shut, I sit on the bed and pull Teddy over to me. "You are, as of now, Teddy Benedictson born in Edmonton, Alberta. And I am Loretta Benedictson. Don't say the other name ever again."

"But why? Can't we ever use our real name again?"

"Benedictson is my real name. I mean, it was my real Dad's name. Bean-Trap put money in the bank here for us under Benedictson, and he must have used that name when he signed into this hotel. So, that's it."

"Oh." He thinks for a minute. "I guess that's what we have to do while we're 'hot', eh Loretta?" he says with a cute grin.

"That's right." I ruffle his hair. "And there's no one hotter in this town right now than Loretta and Teddy Benedictson!"

That night, I take the first long soapy bath I've had since we stayed in the Liberty Hotel. Our house didn't have electricity or running water, so we had to heat water in kettles on the stove to fill the tub. This is luxury! After I've shampooed my hair, I clean up the bathroom and run a tub for Teddy.We have to look good–tomorrow we have a bank job to do, and looks count for everything.

I wash out our clothes, and drape them over the heat registers. When they're partly dry, I lay them flat between the mattresses to press them. No more goose smell!

We pass Eaton's where we bought Teddy's train and my hair ribbons. "Can we go in?" Teddy asks. "I want to see if they have any more Lionel train cars. My Pullman car is smashed."

I have an idea. "If you're really good and remember everything I've told you, and we can get money from the bank account that Dad left for us here, we'll go in and buy a whole new train to replace your old one. Okay?"

"Okay!"

Now comes the hard part. I spot the Imperial Bank of Canada, fronted by big stone steps and heavy glass doors with gold lettering on them. I'm suddenly frightened to death.

"Let's see if Bugs works here," Teddy says.

"Right! We'll ask about him first, before we try to get our money. Maybe he can help us. Barry Nuggs. We'd better not call him Bugs!"

We ask several people if they know Mr. Barry Nuggs before a man with a kind face steps outside his office to help us. "Who is it you're looking for, young lady?" he says.

"Mr. Barry Nuggs," I repeat. "He used to work at a bank on Jasper Avenue, and I thought it might be this one."

"Well, I believe you're in luck," the man says. "Mr. Nuggs is indeed one of our clerks. He works upstairs in our foreign exchange office. I can take you there if you like. Who shall I tell him is inquiring?"

"Loretta and Teddy," I reply.

We follow him up a curving marble staircase to the second floor. Rows of offices with big heavy doors line one side of the floor, while on the other side people work at desks. I see Bugs before the man reaches him, and it's all I can do to stop Teddy, and myself, from running over and hurling ourselves into his arms–very improper behaviour in a bank!

The man goes over to him and points back to the two of us standing behind the railing. Bugs looks puzzled, then a big grin spreads from ear to ear as he recognizes us. "Teddy! Loretta!" he cries, rushing over to us.

"May I take a short break, Mr. Lorimer?" Bugs asks, and the man smiles and nods. Bugs takes us to a room at the back where the staff can eat their lunch, but no one is here in the middle of the morning.

"Tell all," Bugs demands, and sits back to hear our story. But there's one thing I want to know first.

"Bugs, er, Barry," I say, "Jay wrote me that you'd been hurt. Your leg...."

"Yeah, my foot's gone," Barry replies. "Mr. Smith, Jay's dad, had to take it off to save my life. But I now wear a prosthesis, an artificial foot. Look, I can lift my foot up and down, and walk almost normally. The only thing I can't do is turn it from side to side–but who walks on the sides of their feet?" He laughs good-naturedly.

After he hears our story he goes to check out the bank account. When he returns his grin is even broader. "Yep, it's all there, in the name of William Jonathan Benedictson, with signing authority to Loretta Benedictson. I'm going to call my supervisor and explain it all to him."

He tells the supervisor our story, but Bugs adds a surprise ending. "The children's father left this money for their education and well-being. Although Loretta is now fifteen and can legally leave school and be on her own, she and her brother are moving in with my mother and me," Bugs says. I am amazed at how masterful he sounds. Even I believe his story! But what will his mother say? We've never even met her.

"Loretta, er, Benedictson, requires permission from the bank to draw on the interest to pay for their basic requirements, until written authority can be presented from their father, who is...overseas," he says.

"And how!" I say, under my breath.

The supervisor brings in his boss and the three of them talk to us. Teddy and I apparently give all the right answers. Bean-Trap would be proud of how well we can remember things. Finally, I put my signature on a card, and Mr. Lorimer signs it too. We can now take out a monthly allowance. When the business is done, Teddy and I head for the door.

"Hey, where do you think you're going?" Bugs asks.

"Back to our hotel. We're staying at The MacDonald."

Bugs whistles. "You kids like living high on the hog! Okay, I'll meet you there after I finish work. You're staying with us from now on, Mom won't hear of anything else."

"Are you serious? I thought you were saying that just to impress the bank people."

"I'm totally serious! Mom and I live over the dance studio–that's where I got free dance lessons when I was a kid. They'll do the same for you, if you want to learn. I work at nights as a magician. Card tricks are my specialty. And, oh yeah, Mom teaches piano. She'll give you lessons. She loves music and dance. She used to be a can-can girl!" Bugs stops for breath.

Teddy and I laugh. He hasn't changed a bit! I have to interrupt, "Do you still hear from Jay?"

"Oh, yeah! All the time! He's coming here in July, when school's out. His uncle got him a job, loading and off-loading cargo planes for the Fairbanks to Edmonton run. He'll be based here part time, and in Fairbanks part time. Boy, wait until he hears you two are here! He might hitch a plane ride and be down next week!"

I go over to the window and look out onto Jasper Avenue. The street is full of people.Bugs hasn't stopped talking for one second. "...and wait until you meet Frances! "

"Frances?"

"My fiancée! We're getting married next year, she works at the Hudson's Bay store."

Teddy and I leave the bank and walk slowly down Jasper Avenue, like any other Edmonton citizens. But Teddy and I aren't the same as other people, and won't ever be. We're on the run, under false names, the children of a man wanted in two places, possibly for murder. Bugs knows part of our story, but not all of it.

Teddy tugs at my hand. "Loretta, can we go to Eaton's now to look at trains? Maybe they have a stainless-steel streamliner, like the Denver Zephyr. Pretty soon there won't be any more steam locomotives, you know. The conductor told me diesels are the new thing. Someday I might drive a diesel locomotive. Or maybe I'll be a pilot...."

I listen to him prattle on, but in my mind I'm far away from diesels and steam engines, and even from the airplanes that roar overhead. I'm remembering that it's a year ago this week that Mom died, and though so much has happened since then, here we are alone, again.

In my mind I compose a letter to Bean-Trap, coded to hide our identities and location, of course.

Dear Dad:

We've got what you left us. We're living where Teddy got his train, and are going to stay with a friend and his mother. We are also going to go to school. Mom would be proud of us. I know that you will join us soon. But for now, letters will be our only way to keep in touch. Love L and T (and Angel).
XX OO
P.S. We've gambled and won this round. Now, we're betting on you. "Tout va!"

THE END